CAT-ASTROPHIC SPELLS

A Wonder Cats Mystery Book 3

HARPER LIN

ISBN-13: 978-1987859287

ISBN-10: 1987859286

www.harperlin.com

CONTENTS

Soothsayers

oothsayers were not very common among us witches, sort of like redheads with gray eyes. But they might as well have been as common as the name Smith with the way they were portrayed in books and movies. Crystal balls, tea leaves, chicken bones, and a dozen other weird trinkets covered every surface in our homes so we could see the future, which was always filled with tall, dark strangers and long journeys. Right? Not really. In reality, depending on the augur, fortune-telling was either a rare blessing or a curse.

For Aunt Astrid, on the day Levi Cummings came into the café for his reading, it wasn't just a curse. It was a nightmare.

"Go on, honey. It will be fun," Sarah Cummings said to her husband Levi that early Saturday morning. It was the first time Aunt Astrid was doing her Tarot readings in the newly refurbished café.

Aunt Astrid's ability to see the future often made her look as if she were daydreaming or concentrating on a complex puzzle. The fact that she dressed in flowy, colorful, ultra-feminine dresses, wore her graying hair in loose piles on top of her head or a long braid down her back, and smelled of clove made her even more exotic to the locals. Many of them saw her on a monthly basis to get their readings.

However, Levi was not only a newcomer but a skeptic. "Sarah, you know I'm not into this stuff." He rolled his eyes and dropped the newspaper he was reading to take a cautious sip of coffee.

"Just do it for me," Sarah urged. "I'm telling you, you'll be shocked by what she tells you. I just know it."

My cousin Bea was engrossed in the directions for the new cappuccino maker. "This doesn't seem too difficult," she mused.

I usually left that kind of detailed project to her

because reading instructions, following steps in a specific order, and doing things by the book—well, those just weren't my style. Had the installation of the new, state-of-the-art cappuccino maker been left up to me, people would have been getting cups full of steaming hot froth and coffee grounds.

Bea's eyes sparkled with excitement. "So, let's crank this baby up and see what happens."

She snapped on the machine, pulled an espresso shot, and began to steam some milk. I watched, fascinated, as Bea tugged a few levers, pressed a few more buttons, and let the machine growl and gurgle its response. She placed the cup underneath the left spigot, and the foam bubbled out in a perfect peak on top of the cup.

"Here you go." She handed the cup to me.

I smelled the sweetened coffee, raised the cup to my lips, and sipped. "Wow. That tastes good."

She flashed her pretty smile. "You like?" Bea wasn't just my cousin; at two years my junior, she was also my best friend and soul sister.

I nodded as I took another sip.

"Good. Then we can add cappuccino back on the menu. Even though people really should be drinking more tea."

As a healing witch, Bea was very much into the

healing power of healthy diets. That gift was also a blessing and a curse. Since Bea was a hugger by nature, no one ever suspected when she was curing their ailments with a touch. Her actions just came across as a pretty girl being friendly. Had someone paid attention, he would notice that when Bea said hello with a hug or pat, he would leave with a little more spring in his step. But she always lost a little bit of herself in the process. The transfer of energy gave the recipient a nice boost.

"I'm waiting for the day we add double cheese-burgers to the menu." I didn't look up from my cup as I set it on the counter.

"That reminds me. We are almost out of kale for the Green Fiend salads."

A shiver ran down my spine. *Kale.* How did that vegetable ever catch on? I grimaced. "I'll add it to the shopping list."

I looked up at the Cummings. Levi was still reading the paper.

Sarah nervously glanced over her shoulder at Aunt Astrid then muttered to her husband, "Well, I booked a ten o'clock session with her, and it's now three minutes after. If you don't want to do it, you need to tell her so she doesn't waste her time waiting. We can go ahead and get to that sports store you like for those thingies for your tennis racket."

Sarah looked down at her fingernails as if they held something fascinating then focused her attention out the window, avoiding her husband's face altogether.

Levi peeked at her over his newspaper and grinned. "Oh, all right. I'm going, I'm going." He folded up the paper and stood.

Sarah's face instantly lit up. "Really, Levi. Get ready to be amazed."

"Yeah, yeah." He kissed his wife on the top of her head on his way to the back of the café.

The new Brew-Ha-Ha had a nice long counter that I liked to work behind because it gave me a view of everyone coming and going. It was made of beautiful dark wood that Aunt Astrid and Bea had sanded and stained themselves. There were a dozen cozy wooden tables with mismatched wooden chairs scattered throughout the comfy dining area. The walls were painted a deep red, and we had splurged on vintage pictures of romantic old castles against vivid green landscapes and fluffy cats lounging on thick, plush pillows.

We could have been a cliché and had stereotypical pointy-hat-wearing, broom-toting, cauldron-stirring sages placed around, but we didn't want to advertise. No one in town knew we were witches. They thought Aunt Astrid might have been a medium, but I often heard people comment that she wasn't as good as the woman from New Jersey who contacted the dead on television.

And that was just fine with us. Witches have never been all that well-received throughout history. My thought was: *if it ain't broke, don't fix it*. It was better to keep our family secret exactly that… secret.

The kitchen was around the counter to the right. Our new baker, Kevin, was busy making something from Aunt Astrid's recipe box that smelled delicious.

To the left, a single booth was recessed into the wall to look like one of those romantic alcoves at fancy restaurants that were reserved for couples who wanted to be out in public yet secluded. The small area was painted a golden yellow and had sheer navy curtains draping either side of the threshold.

Aunt Astrid did her fortune telling in the alcove. She didn't have a crystal ball or anything. She would just have her guest sit down across from her and hold her hands. Then she would talk with them and let the images and hints of the future come to her.

"Have fun, Levi," I said as he passed.

Bea took the opportunity to sit with Sarah and chitchat for a few minutes.

I scanned the dining area. A dude with long hair, glasses, and ear buds dangling from his ears stared at his laptop, his head bobbing to some beat only he could hear. An older man with wrinkled skin was reading a good, old-fashioned book with a steaming hot mug of coffee next to him. Two college-aged girls talked as fast as birds chirping at sunrise.

I took a deep breath and stretched, then nearly jumped out of my skin when I turned to find Levi standing at the end of the counter and looking pale and sweaty. "Are you all right?" I asked.

He nodded slightly but didn't look at me. He slowly walked up to Sarah, who had her back to him.

Bea looked over Sarah's head, and the words stopped in her mouth. "Levi?"

Sarah turned around in her seat. Her face instantly transformed into a mask of worry. "Honey?"

"I think I need to get home," Levi said quietly.

Sarah stood and placed her hand on his arm. "You look like you've seen a ghost. Do you want to sit down?" Her eyes darted to mine then Bea's. "For heaven's sake, what did she tell you?"

He shook his head. "No, Sarah. It wasn't the fortune. I just suddenly feel out of sorts."

I quickly poured a glass of water and whisked around the counter. "Take a load off, Levi. Here." I held out the glass. "Drink this."

"Yes, Levi. Please sit down," Bea added. I could tell she wanted to place her hand on him to see what exactly was the matter.

But he flinched away from her, and she missed her opportunity. "No. Sarah, get me home." His voice was soft.

Suddenly, I remembered Aunt Astrid. I turned, and in a few long strides, I was back at the cozy alcove, looking at my aunt, who was shaking her head and chewing her lip thoughtfully.

"Aunt Astrid, are you okay? My gosh, Levi Cummings looks like you clobbered him over the head with news worse than cancer. He doesn't have cancer, right? Oh, please tell me it's not cancer."

"It's not cancer. In fact, I didn't get a chance to tell him anything. He told me."

I looked back at the dining room and saw Bea on her way toward me. "How about you? Did you get a chance to diagnose him?" I asked.

She shook her head and looked at her mother.

"Are you okay?" She slipped into the booth and placed her hand on her mom's arm.

"I'm completely fine. Except…"

"Except what?" I shifted from my right foot to my left.

Aunt Astrid took a deep breath and looked around the back area of the café, past me, past Bea, and into a realm we couldn't see. Her lips drew down, and her eyebrows inched closer together while her eyes squinted. She swallowed hard then looked at us.

"Someone is being murdered, now, this very minute."

"What?" I asked skeptically.

"Why would you say that, Mom?" Bea asked.

"Levi told me," Aunt Astrid explained. "Well, it wasn't Levi. I doubt Levi has any idea that he said anything. I'll bet he thinks he was just struck by some unexplainable migraine, nothing more." Still, her eyes wandered.

"Wait. Are you telling me that Levi Cummings, the guy who sells carpet, channeled some spiritual informant and gave you a tip on a murder? Did he say who? Should we call the police?"

"Hold on, Cath. Mom, what exactly happened?"

With a forlorn look on her face, Aunt Astrid told us her story.

Before Levi had even decided to come back and have his fortune told, Aunt Astrid could sense something had accompanied him into the café because of a shift in the air. It was as if a breeze gently blowing a spiral spider web had moved the dimensions she could see. She sat very still, waiting for whatever was causing the ripples to show itself.

"Hi," he said pleasantly. "I'm—"

"Levi. I know." Aunt Astrid smiled. Apparently, that gave Levi a bit of a start, so she added, "Your wife made the appointment for you."

"Oh, yes, she did. She thought I'd enjoy it." Tentatively, he scooted into the booth.

Aunt Astrid stretched out her hands, and as soon as his skin touched hers, everything changed.

Levi's eyes rolled over white. His body went rigid, and he held onto Aunt Astrid's wrists with a tight grip. He opened his mouth as if he expected a doctor to place a tongue depressor inside and ask him to say "ahh," then froze.

The words that came out of him were not from his own vocal cords. They weren't even from a person. They were from somewhere else. And there had been many of them.

Aunt Astrid shook her head at us. "But I could hear each one as clear as my own voice right now."

"What did they say?" I asked, not sure I really wanted to know.

"'She's killing him, you know. She's killing him because he told her no. He's dying right now. And she'll get away with it, too.'"

"Did you ask him who?" Bea asked.

"Yes, but it was too late. Levi's eyes snapped back to normal. He closed his mouth, began to sweat, rubbed his head, then just said sorry and excused himself. I didn't dare tell him he had been channeling."

"Right," I said.

"Maybe it isn't true," Bea said. "I mean, we have no name, no location. This could have been a transmission he tapped into from another part of the country, or the world even. Maybe it was a delayed inter-dimensional echo, something that happened a decade ago that just bounced off the café walls today."

"No," Aunt Astrid said. "This happened here and now. I am sure of it. Before Levi even sat down, I saw the waves. Something was pushing its way through the layers of astral plains to get to us, here, at this moment, in this place. I'll bet we'll hear of a murder in town before the day is over."

"So what do we do?" I asked. "Just wait around?"

"What would you suggest?" Aunt Astrid asked, leaning back into the soft padding of the booth. "We can't very well go door to door. And I wouldn't advise calling the police. The last thing we want to do is draw attention to ourselves. Not to mention cause any unnecessary worry for Jake. If he knew we knew something about this…" Aunt Astrid and I looked at Bea. "Well, it could cause unnecessary problems."

Bea nodded. Jake, Bea's husband, was a detective for the Wonder Falls police department. He had just started coming around to the fact that he was married to a witch, his mother-in-law was a witch, and her cousin was a witch. That was a lot for any man to take in, and we didn't want to rush him.

I untied my apron and folded it neatly, getting ready to make my getaway and start snooping around. "You're right. Maybe Treacle has heard something?"

Treacle was my cat. He was a beautiful black cat that roamed the streets like a lion, proud and dangerous if need be. We communicated by telepathy, which was my gift, and I saw no downside to it.

"Have you seen him this morning?" Bea asked.

I shook my head. "He slipped out two nights ago. I'd have heard if he was in any trouble. I'll call him while I go for a walk. Think this whole thing through a little bit."

"Okay," Aunt Astrid said. I could tell she was mulling over the whole incident.

Bea was also a little preoccupied as she scooted out of the booth and took my hand. She pulled me to the front of the café. "Tell Marshmallow not to mention anything to Peanut Butter. He'd just worry, okay?" Bea said, wringing her hands.

Marshmallow was Aunt Astrid's fluffy white cat. She used to belong to a magician, and she was the most powerful of all of our cats. Peanut Butter was Bea's young, brown cat.

"Of course. I'll be back before the lunch crowd."

WALKING THROUGH THE NEIGHBORHOOD, I called out to Treacle in my mind, focusing on the animal shelter Old Murray Willis ran. Treacle usually turned up there. I got no response. For a second, I felt a twinge of worry.

Under normal circumstances, I wouldn't give it a second thought. Treacle was a wanderer, like the hobos who rode the rails during the Depression. I could say with a country twang the highway was his home. Yet the idea of something pushing its way through the dimensions to get us a message freaked me out just a little. I would have been better able to focus if I knew my favorite feline was okay.

Then, I saw a familiar sight. The siren of Jake's unmarked squad car beeped at me in salutation. It was just my luck he had his partner with him, Blake Samberg. Jake and Blake, the detective duo.

Blake was a serious, no-nonsense, by-the-book, just-the-facts-ma'am kind of detective, and he had little time for anything else. On his days off, he probably did nothing but sit around watching old film noir movies and practice brooding in front of the mirror.

I walked up to the car as it swerved to the curb. Bending over, I leaned through the window.

"Hey, Cath." Jake's smile looked a little tired.

"Hi, Jake. What are you two guys up to?" I looked around again, searching for Treacle.

"Responding to a 419," Blake said, barely looking up from his notepad.

"Care to translate for Mr. Manners over there, Jake?" I jerked my chin in Blake's direction, but he didn't give me the courtesy of looking up to see my eye rolling or my smirking. He just kept looking at his notes.

"A 419 is a dead body," Jake said.

I hoped my expression didn't give me away. Judging by Jake's response, he didn't notice I was just a little more than interested.

"My gosh," I murmured. "Not a good way to start the day for you guys." I swallowed. "Was it natural causes?"

"We don't know yet. The place was neat, but there were a few bits of weirdness, and the body had no signs of outside trauma. Actually"—Jake patted my arm—"I shouldn't be telling you this. You'll have nightmares."

"I'm two years older than your wife. Nothing scares me, except maybe that mug over there." I nodded in Blake's direction. He still didn't look up, but his pen stopped moving.

Jake chuckled. "So what's got you out and about? You got the day off?"

"No. I just took my break early to see if I could find Treacle. He's on the loose again. I haven't seen him in two days." My voice was casual, but I couldn't help the slight tremor in it. I hoped I hadn't sounded too interested in all the gory details of the 419.

"That big old alley cat will be back. He knows where the food is. That's usually what brings the drifters back home. It's easier than chasing mice and working for a meal."

Nodding, I looked over the top of the car anxiously—not to find Treacle, but because I wanted to get back to the café and tell Aunt Astrid and Bea about the new information I'd learned. Except Jake didn't say it was a murder. He'd just said it was a dead body.

"You're probably right. I should get back to the café, anyway. We've got inventory to do. We need more flour and kale, and I think I'm going to get extra chocolates from Sweetie's across town. You know that Marvin makes the greatest toffee you've ever tasted. The stuff won't stay in the display for—"

"I hate to say it, Cath," Blake interrupted. "But you won't be getting any more chocolates from Marvin. He was our 419."

My mouth fell open. "You're kidding."

Just as I was about to press them for more information, the police radio crackled to life. A female dispatcher called for any unit in the vicinity to report to something going on a couple of blocks away.

"Sorry, Cath," Jake said. "We gotta run. Tell Bea I'll call her later."

I nodded and stepped away from the car. It

quickly pulled away as Blake placed the red bulb on his side of the roof.

Hurrying back to the café, I continued to call Treacle in my mind, but I wasn't shouting as loudly as I should have been. I was distracted. Jake had said there were no marks on Marvin. Maybe the poor guy just had a heart attack. But what had Jake meant by there being weird things around Marvin's house?

I hustled back to the café for the lunchtime rush. I grabbed my apron and hopped behind the counter. I thought I was going to explode with my news.

"Have I got to talk to *you*," I said to Bea in between running the register and making out the list of necessities we needed at the counter. Kevin was very particular about the ingredients he used for Aunt Astrid's recipes, so thankfully, I was able to stay clear of the massive pantry in the back.

"Oh, yeah?" she asked, looking intrigued. "Can't wait."

We worked together like two parts of the same machine in an effort to get everyone fed and taken care of. The clock ticked, and every minute seemed to creep by at a snail's pace. Finally, around two o'clock, the café was empty enough that I could corral Aunt Astrid and Bea together out of earshot of the remaining customers. I told them everything Jake had said.

"I don't believe it," Bea said. "Marvin was a nice man, and I'll tell you what, I don't recall him having any kind of heart trouble. In fact, aside from a bit of a spare tire and bifocals, the guy was in good shape both physically and spiritually. Still a little sadness over his wife passing away a few years back, but nothing out of the ordinary. Nothing that would kill him."

"Now, girls, just because Jake happened to mention this doesn't mean it is *our* murder," Aunt Astrid said. "It could just be an unfortunate coincidence."

I looked around at the few remaining customers. "Aunt Astrid, you might not want to say the words 'our murder' too loudly. People might overhear and get the wrong idea, you know?"

No one really seemed to be paying any attention to us. I thanked Kevin for that. His cooking was mesmerizing, and the aromas filled the entire café with warm waves of deliciousness. Murder or no murder, I was going to get a slice of the German chocolate cake he was baking before the day was over.

"Well, if you both can hang on until tonight,

Cath, you've given me a perfect excuse to bring it up to Jake. I'll see what I can find out," Bea said.

Aunt Astrid handed each of us a rag. "Until then, we should just go on with things as normal."

Taking the hint, we began to wipe down the tables. I thought it was hard waiting to tell them what Jake had told me. It was even harder waiting for Jake to get home and Bea to find out the rest of the story.

The rest of the day dragged, and staring at the phone after I got home didn't help. Bea finally called at a little after nine o'clock. I took the phone out to my backyard. The air was cool, and the cicadas sang a haunting tune. After I answered, Bea told me I needed to get to the café right away.

Sweetie's

❧❦❧

The café was dark when I got there. I knocked on the glass door, and within a few seconds, Bea hustled up from the basement. She flipped the bolt then yanked open the door.

"Thank goodness you're here. Come on." Taking my hand, she pulled me into the shadowy restaurant and around the counter to the concrete basement steps. The little bunker was sort of like our clubhouse, where we could meet and talk freely about… well, in this case, murder.

Aunt Astrid handed me a cup of tea she'd heated on her little hotplate. Bea could barely contain herself, and I saw she had a cup of tea she hadn't even touched. For her to let an all-natural herbal remedy sit untouched meant she must have some-thing big on her mind.

"When Jake came home, I just casually mentioned that you'd said you ran into him. I thought I was going to have to do a lot of tip-toeing around the topic, but as it turned out, he was ready to talk."

I took a seat on the soft imitation Oriental rug that covered the concrete floor, folding my legs underneath me. "What did he say?" I carefully set my teacup down in front of me. It wouldn't be long before the tea became cold. I was so shocked, I didn't sip a drop as she told me everything.

The call had come into the Wonder Falls Police Station almost the minute after Levi had left the Brew-Ha-Ha Café. A frantic woman screamed and cried into the phone that she had found her father on the floor of his home, and he was not responding.

When the paramedics arrived, they found Brit Clegg near hysterics next to her father Marvin Clegg who lay in the middle of the living room floor. From what the EMTs could see, the first level of the house was torn apart. It hadn't just been ransacked by a junkie looking for drugs or money. The place looked violated, purposefully vandalized.

Some pictures had been ripped in half while

others remained untouched. The seat cushions looked as though they had been clawed open. Weird graffiti was scribbled on the walls with both marker and spray paint. A grimace on the dead man's face made it obvious he'd been in great pain or fear when he died. The paramedics had estimated he'd been dead for a couple of hours.

"Jake said it broke his heart to see the ambulance drivers wheel that sheet-covered body out of the house with the daughter still sobbing on the floor. She kept crying 'Daddy, oh Daddy,'" Bea said. "It took him almost twenty minutes to get her to stand and step out onto the porch for questioning."

"Did he think she had something to do with it?" I cleared my throat as I pushed the image of my own mother out of my mind. Days went by in which I didn't consciously think of her on that terrible night. But as sure as the sun rose in the east, I would see those giant monster hands pulling her underneath my bed and hear her voice at least once every day. I'd be back on top of my bed in my pink nightgown, eleven years old, screaming for help that didn't come in time. I assumed my mother was dead. Whatever it was she'd fought off had wanted me, and I was pretty sure it wasn't to play dolls. Instead, it took my mom, and I was left all alone.

Sure, I had Bea and Aunt Astrid, and I loved them with all my heart. They were my family. They believed my story about a monster under the bed dragging my mother away. But no matter who you were, when your parents passed, you'd prefer they simply fell asleep peacefully in the house where you grew up, surrounded by family and friends. Anything other than that was… unnatural. And all too real.

My eye stung as a single tear tried to surface, but I blinked it back.

Bea's voice shifted from factual to sympathetic. "Jake said they weren't ruling anything out. They were going to wait a couple of days and call her back into the station. He was going to let Blake question her."

I finally took a sip of my tea and cringed a little at the ice-cold flavor of "green." "Well, that ought to scare a confession out of her. Was it for money?"

Aunt Astrid looked down at me from the soft, green chair she had moved into the basement for herself. "Aren't you being a little judgmental?"

I defiantly sipped more of the cold tea. "I don't know. Am I? Levi did say *she*, didn't he? And the chocolate business was making a pretty penny, right? I mean, I know what they were charging us for a couple dozen boxes of chocolate-covered toffee. They certainly couldn't have been starving."

Aunt Astrid looked past me to the highlights and shadows only she could see. "It doesn't look good for the girl, but something is telling me it isn't that easy. I can't put my finger on it."

"Well, they guessed the cause of death was a heart attack. A real bad one," Bea said. "But they'll know for sure after the autopsy."

"So I guess we just wait and see. We might be able to sit this one out and let the cops handle it. Let Blake work his own special brand of magic." I chuckled at my own clever play on words.

"I wish we could. But Jake gave me this." Bea took a crumpled piece of paper from her front blouse pocket and handed it to Aunt Astrid, who gasped.

"What?" I mumbled, narrowing my eyes. "What is it?" Aunt Astrid handed me the paper, and it was my turn to gasp. "I know what these are. Not all of them, but I know what some of them are. Where did Jake get these?"

She swallowed hard. "He said they were all over the walls. He quickly drew them as best he could because he thought I might know what they meant. He couldn't very well get us the crime scene photos."

Scrawled in thin, blue ballpoint lines were bizarre symbols and letters from a long forgotten alphabet. The markings were crude, and some weren't even correct, making nonsensical commands if translated literally.

"This is… it looks like a third-grader did this," I said. "Am I looking at this right? A cessation summons?"

Bea shrugged. "Taking Jake's artistic abilities into account, I thought that same thing myself."

"Are we sure he drew them right? If you don't know this stuff and leave out a line here or there, it looks close enough, to a non-witch. But to us witches, it can read totally different."

"I asked him, and he said he drew them exactly the way they were."

Aunt Astrid chewed her bottom lip thoughtfully. "The problem with this assumption is that we are reading this with witches' eyes and a little bit of information the police do not know… Levi's tip. Those scrawlings could be a summons, or they could be a random act of vandalism. The difference between the two is negligible."

"I hate to say this," Bea said. "But I need to see the body."

"Did you ask Jake?" I was surprised Bea was even

making such a suggestion. It was a little on the morbid side for her.

"I didn't." She bit her lower lip. "I know the body is at the coroner's office right now."

Aunt Astrid looked seriously at Bea. "Are you sure you want to see it? You and Jake have been working so hard on things together. You don't want to start with any secrets again, do you?"

"No, but… I have a feeling in my gut," Bea said.

"You could blame me," I offered. "Lord knows it wouldn't be the first time I got you in trouble."

Bea chuckled. "I couldn't do that."

"Sure you could."

Aunt Astrid stood and began to sift through a small stack of books she'd brought from her house. "You guys are talking like walking into the coroner's office at this hour of the night is the easy part. Even if Jake knew about it, he can't just take you in there to see a body."

"I don't know, Mom. Something isn't right with those symbols that Jake wrote down. If he or Blake gets any closer and we do nothing, it could turn out badly."

Picking up what looked like a child's cardboard book, Aunt Astrid cleared her throat. "I might be able to help. But the sooner we get this over with, the better." She studied the thick pages without looking at us. "We have some time. Levi gave us that. This hasn't made the news yet, so any traces of a cessation summons, or of any witchcraft, may still be left behind."

"Unless we are dealing with a *diabolist*." A shiver ran up my spine.

"You don't really think it could be that?" Bea asked, shaking her head. "Do you?"

When Aunt Astrid didn't say "Oh, no. Stop being silly," I wished I hadn't mentioned it.

"Let's get our facts straight before we start guessing. Bea, do you have any idea how you might get into the coroner's office?" I would follow my family to the ends of the earth, but the idea of seeing a dead body brought back memories of the ones haphazardly exhumed at the cemetery not so long ago.

Poor Marvin. Instead of thinking of his wonderful candies, I would be waiting for his eyes to pop open, for him to pull himself clumsily off the table and stagger toward us, arms outstretched, gurgling horrifically.

"Well, what do you say?" Bea asked, looking at me.

"To what?"

"To going to the coroner's office and causing a distraction?"

"What?"

"I thought I could pretend to bring Jake a late-night snack."

"Is Jake going to be there?"

"No. He's at the station. I already know that."

"If he's not there, then why would you bring him a snack?"

"When they say he isn't there, I'll just ask to use the bathroom, slip into the autopsy room, and get a quick peek."

"And what am I supposed to do?"

"Keep the guard talking. Flirt, or ask a lot of questions." Bea was smiling and nodding. "Dazzle whoever it is with your sparkling personality."

I rolled my eyes. "Fine. I'm in. It'll give me a chance to keep an eye out for Treacle, too."

"He still hasn't come home?" Aunt Astrid's voice was a little worried.

I shook my head.

"He's a smart cat. He'll be back," she soothed.

I hoped she was right. Even though he had disappeared for longer periods of time before, I was starting to worry.

Bea reached down, took my hands, and hoisted

me up. "Grab a paper bag on your way up, and I'll grab some snacks."

"For what?" I asked.

"We can't say we're bringing Jake a snack and not have a snack."

I slapped my head. I was glad Bea was taking the lead because my mind didn't seem to be in it. Thoughts of Treacle distracted me. I didn't want to admit how worried I was, and my unease was affecting my concentration.

I confided my fears to Bea. "I just have a different feeling this time, Bea. Usually, I can call to Treacle and get a couple of clicks or squeaks to let me know he's heard me and is okay. This time, it's like shouting into a cave and hearing my own voice echo back to me."

"Did he tell you anything when he left?"

"No. He just wanted out for the night like usual."

Bea gently patted my back. "We'll keep an eye out for him. I'm sure he's okay."

As we slipped out the front door of the café, we didn't see a soul on our side of the street. Across the way, a boy rode his bike in wobbly patterns then began pumping his legs faster as he sped away. Down the block, we heard a couple talking as they climbed into a car. The chirp-chirp of the car doors being unlocked echoed down the street, followed by the car doors slamming as the couple got in and drove off.

"Are you scared?" I asked Bea.

"I'll be a lot more scared if I don't find out what we're dealing with."

"I hope they don't close down Sweetie's. Where would we get our chocolates?"

Bea rolled her eyes at me. "Really? You're worried about the chocolates?"

"I'm not trying to be disrespectful. It's just that those were some darn good chocolates."

"They were."

"Do you think there's an angle there? Someone after the business?"

"That's what Jake was saying. But he didn't elaborate very much."

At this time of night, the streets were quiet. We drove to the coroner's office in a little over five minutes. The building was a friendly-looking place. Considering most people went there under painful circumstances, the city did its best to give it a positive and peaceful appearance.

I especially liked the colorful flowers flanking each side of the entrance. I could never get anything to grow like that. I had two cacti in my kitchen window that reached about four inches in height then decided that was enough.

Quickly, we went over our plan.

"Got it?" Bea asked, her eyes serious.

"Yeah, I guess. Let's do it."

A Grump

❧

Bea and I walked up to the building, and the automatic sliding glass doors swooshed open. We probably looked like a couple of kooks strolling in there, and I made a mental note of the cameras recording us. We hadn't thought of those.

Closing my eyes, I mumbled a vision spell that might, just might, cause a temporary camera malfunction long enough to keep us out of view. It was sort of like pulling a little extra electricity from the air into one concentrated spot.

Bea glanced at me, and I knew she could smell it. The act of the vision spell gave off a slight odor as if a storm were coming. That smell would probably be what the front desk clerk would remember, too.

"Can I help you ladies?" the man at the reception desk asked. He was wearing the uniform of Wonder Falls' finest, and the name on the desk plate read Stephen Ferdeck. His name was familiar, but I couldn't place him.

"Hi, Officer. I'm Bea Williams, Detective Jake Williams's wife. Is he here?"

Officer Ferdeck looked at us as if we had suddenly turned green. "No, Mrs. Williams. He isn't here. He's at the station. Do you want me to ring him there?" His eyes shifted back and forth from me to Bea suspiciously.

"Oh no, I'm sorry. He had mentioned something he had to deal with today, and it seemed to bother him, so I brought him a little treat to keep his spirits up."

Again, Officer Ferdeck didn't budge an inch.

"Well, we're sorry to bother you. I hate to ask this, but... would it be possible to use the ladies' room? I should have gone before I left. You were right, Cath." She looked at me then rolled her eyes back at the officer. "Too much green tea." She giggled uncomfortably.

"Sure," Officer Ferdeck said. "Restrooms are right over there." He nodded toward the restrooms behind us. They were nowhere near the autopsy room.

I cocked my right hip and folded my arms across my chest. "Yeah, you should have gone at the café, Bea."

Bea shrugged. Just as we turned toward the restroom, a car pulled up in front of the building. The high beams poured through the glass, and Bea cleared her throat. We had both seen the familiar unmarked vehicle a million times. The lights shut off, and the car door slammed.

Blake Samberg came through the sliding doors. Then *he* looked at us suspiciously. I don't think a plan had ever gone more wrong. "Evening, Stephen," he grumbled in his typical brooding voice. "Bea? Cath? What brings you two here?"

"Is Jake with you?" Bea asked, her voice masking her nervousness. She was a much better actor than me. I'd have liked to tell the detective to mind his own business, even though I knew I had "guilty of something" written all over my face.

"No, Bea. He's wrapping up some paperwork at the office. Do you need him?"

"No, no. I must have heard him wrong and thought he was going to be here tonight. I brought him a little treat from the café." Bea stepped up to Blake and in a hushed voice said, "I heard about the man you brought in today. I'm so sorry."

Blake, whose features never changed when he spoke to me, seemed to soften slightly. "Yeah. It was disturbing. It looked like some kind of witchcraft, hoodoo-voodoo nonsense in that house. I'm actually here to pick up some of the paperwork on that very case."

"Witchcraft?" I asked as my eyes darted from Bea to Blake. "Do you have any knowledge of that? I mean, any formal training or anything that would make you think that? It's kind of jumping the gun, don't you think?" I couldn't help myself. The words just came out. So many misconceptions existed about witches and witchcraft. I sometimes had a hard time controlling my tongue.

"No, I don't. But thankfully, it won't be hard to find out. It was a very rough scene, as I'm sure Jake mentioned." He blew me off as if I were an annoying fly to be swatted away.

"No, he didn't go into detail. He usually doesn't." Bea glared at me. "Blake, I'm wondering if I can ask a very big favor?" She placed her hand gently on Blake's shoulder and turned him away from Stephen and me.

They whispered to each other then Blake nodded. He walked over to Stephen and said something quietly so I couldn't hear. Apparently, I was being left out of this particular game of telephone. I was annoyed.

Stephen reached underneath his desk and pressed a button. The doors leading to the autopsy room opened.

"Where you going?" I asked Bea innocently.

"I'll be right back," she said in a quiet voice. I looked at Blake, who was staring at me oddly. I couldn't say how it was odd, just that it was. I wondered what Bea had said to him.

Stephen looked at me as Bea and Blake headed toward the autopsy room. A few awkward moments passed, and I walked a couple of paces back and forth, trying to casually escape the gaze of Stephen, whose name was familiar even though I couldn't place his face.

He kept staring at me.

"So, what's your problem?" I asked. "You've been looking at me like you've seen my face up at the post office. What's the matter?"

"You're Cath Greenstone, aren't you?"

"Yes, I am. Have we met before?"

"Not formally. But I know *of* you."

My eyebrows shot up. Did I have some kind of torrid reputation I was blissfully unaware of?

"And truthfully, I don't like you," he said. The

statement from a stranger felt like a punch in the gut.

"You don't like me? You don't even know me!"

"Oh, I know you. You were never nice in high school, and from the looks of things, you are still a grade-A grump." His body never moved. He didn't shift in his seat. Only his lips moved as he spoke, and his eyes followed me.

Raising my hand to my chest, I couldn't contain my awkward giggle. "High school? A grump?"

"Well, another word comes to mind, but out of respect for my deceased mother, I won't say it... but it rhymes with ditch."

For a second, I thought this mystery man from my youth knew my secret until I realized there was a word that might fit the bill besides witch. I felt a little stupid. "Can you tell me what I did? I'm not trying to be rude or anything. It's just that high school was a long time ago. I didn't have a very good go of it myself."

Stephen took a deep breath then looked up at me. "You ran for class president our sophomore year."

"Yeah, and I lost... by a lot."

"If you hadn't run, there would have only been two candidates—me against Paula Lipinski."

"So what? I was doing it just to see what would happen. I didn't expect to really win. I just wanted to conduct a social experiment of sorts. Have a little fun stirring things up."

"You were like the Ralph Nader of our sophomore class. Because of you, I lost the election. Who knows how much differently my life would have turned out if it weren't for you?"

I stood there in shock. A high school election has bothered this guy all this time? Was he just sitting around hoping someday I'd stroll into the coroner's office so he could give me a hard time? "Stephen Ferdeck for President: Not Your Mama's Candidate." That was his slogan. The memory came rushing back to me, and I smiled. "You had the best slogan!"

He looked at me oddly. "What are you talking about?"

"'Not Your Mama's Candidate'? That was you, right?"

He thought for a moment, then his eyes brightened.

"It was more creative than mine." I rolled my eyes. "'Cath Greenstone: Why Not?'"

I laughed. My high school days were not fun. I ran for class president my sophomore year on a dare from my best friend Min. If it weren't for him, high school would have been unbearable. As Stephen Ferdeck had said, who knew how much differently my life would have turned out if it weren't for Min. But the memory of our slogans sneaked up on me, and I had to laugh.

Stephen was also beginning to laugh. "I had forgotten that."

"Yeah, you were so caught up in me throwing a wrench into your candidacy, you forgot the best part of your campaign. What did Paula Lipinski use? See, I don't even remember. I had totally forgotten about her until you brought her up."

A smile started to form on Officer Stephen Ferdeck's face. I couldn't help but smile back.

"Officer Ferdeck, I'm sorry. If you have been holding that in all these years and feel I ruined your future, I am truly sorry. You look to be doing pretty good from where I'm standing right now."

"I do love my job," he said reluctantly.

"Well, let me make it up to you." I folded my arms over my chest and pretended to think hard. "Do you know the Brew-Ha-Ha Café across town?"

He thought for a moment then nodded. "That place burned down, didn't it?"

"Oh, yeah." It was common knowledge the café had experienced a bad fire.

"I didn't realize it had reopened."

Nodding, I shifted from one foot to the other. "Well, I own the café with Bea and my Aunt Astrid. How about you come in and visit? We can reminisce about high school, and lunch and coffee will be on me. We just hired a fantastic new baker, and he makes everything from scratch."

He smiled and blinked. "I'm vegan. Does that make a difference?"

I rolled my eyes. "Seriously? Well, no, it doesn't make a difference. Bea is very educated when it comes to feeding the body and soul, so I'm pretty confident we can accommodate."

He stuck out his hand to shake. I walked up and obliged. "Thanks, Cath. I'm sorry I called you grumpy, and… you know."

"Hey, I've been called worse. I can't say you're that far off the mark."

Just then, Bea emerged from the autopsy room with Blake following her. They were talking in hushed voices, and when I looked at Bea's pale face, I instantly became worried.

"Thank you, Detective. I am grateful," she said, shaking Blake's hand. She took a wobbly step toward me and slipped her arm through mine, gently urging me toward the front sliding doors.

"What is the matter with you?" I asked urgently. "Are you all right?"

"Just get me to the car. We've got to get home."

Exploding Heart

I waved to Officer Ferdeck and gave Blake a slightly concerned look. He knew something but wasn't telling me. And I knew something but wasn't telling him. We were both looking down the same scary tunnel.

Bea held onto me tightly as we walked to her car.

"So? What did you find out?" My voice echoed off the three cars in the parking lot, the garbage dumpster, and the brick walls of the coroner's office. We were totally alone, but I worried someone might overhear us.

"It was a mess in there, Cath." We climbed into the car. Bea sat behind the wheel and took a couple of deep breaths. "I barely touched the body. When I walked in, I could see the metaphysical residue from what had happened to him all over. It was thick and black, and there were globs of...stuff...so thick, it was piling on the floor. Even though it was only me who could see it, I swear Blake knew something was there. He stood back from the table, like he was afraid he might get some of it on him."

I took a deep breath. "Maybe he's just squeamish around carcasses. I can't say I don't know how that feels," I said quietly, as if dismissing Blake's behavior could somehow change what Bea had seen.

"No. He was onto something. I could tell he could feel it."

I cleared my throat and looked through the windshield at the bushes in front of us. A thick, soft, piney type of foliage bordered the small parking lot. For a second, I half expected to see something peeking back at me from the pitch-black shadows. But there was nothing.

"And Cath, that isn't even the worst part." Bea turned her head and looked at me with tears in her eyes. "He didn't just die of a heart attack."

"What did he die of?"

"His heart exploded inside his chest."

I was speechless. What do you say to that kind of news? "So, the cessation summons?"

"Oh, it's definitely a witch doing this. This was a pitiful attempt at a cessation summons. But whoever did this, he or she isn't very good. They made a mess of everything."

I had never seen Bea so upset. She was squeezing and kneading the steering wheel as she spoke. "Obviously they didn't expect anyone in Wonder Falls to be privy to the realm of spells and magic." Bea wiped away the tear that had snuck down her cheek.

"Well, was there any kind of clue or tip to point us in the right direction? Marvin knew a lot of people. I mean, his candy was shipped all over the country. What if he crossed someone who lives in New York or Florida, and we are all the way over here? How could we ever hope to narrow down the search, let alone catch them?"

Bea slowly shook her head. "It's not a local person, but they are located here now. Inside all the mystical goo and filth that they left all over the body, I sensed a transference spell. I couldn't pinpoint the location without giving Blake something unnatural to contemplate telling Jake, so I did what I could with what I was given to work with. It came from somewhere on the west side."

"Well, that is better than nothing, right? Even

though the west side is a couple miles in all directions."

Bea started the car and put it in reverse. "Don't be so negative. We need to talk to my mom."

We arrived at Aunt Astrid's house a few minutes past ten. After letting ourselves in, we found her sitting cross-legged on the floor surrounded by towers of books. And of course, Marshmallow was sprawled across an open book, her tail waving lazily at us when we walked in.

Bea took center stage and repeated to her mom what she had told me: the gross residue, the amateurish technique, the transference spell directing us to the west side, plus Jake's discreet information regarding the weird writing on the walls.

"Yeah, what about all that stuff?" I had to ask how it got all over the walls. Why would a witch make a man's heart explode in his chest from a distance yet take the risk of being seen at the crime scene and leaving crucial evidence? It didn't make any sense.

Sounds like trouble, Marshmallow said to me telepathically, looking up and licking her paw as I scratched the top of her head.

"I'll bet if we were to go back to that house, all those sketches and symbols would be gone," Aunt Astrid said. "You said this was done from a distance. I believe that. And those images were just an attempt to scare the victim. They emerged from the wall as they were uttered by the witch. But I'll bet they're gone now. This person, who is so magically sloppy and careless, decided to show off a little to Marvin. 'Look at what I can do. I can scare you. I can cause you pain. I can kill you. I am in charge.'"

I was still worried about narrowing down the search. "So you don't think this was like a loan-shark arrangement gone bad, or a union dispute or something?"

"Not at all," Aunt Astrid said. "That wouldn't make sense. I don't think loan sharks deal in witch-craft. And as far as I've heard, the Teamsters don't have a clause allowing for heart explosions in their contracts."

Laughing a little, I could see Aunt Astrid's point.

"No." Her eyes narrowed. "This was personal. Whoever did this wanted to make sure Marvin took notice of them immediately. My guess is that he didn't move fast enough for them."

"Well, we know it's magic. We know it is an

amateur trying to do what I'd call 'big girl magic.' And this person killed Marvin intentionally. Who would have a motive like that?" I thought out loud.

Bea scratched the side of her head. "He didn't have any business partners. He grew Sweetie's with his own hands, so I don't think it was over the business."

"His wife died years ago," Aunt Astrid said.

"Yeah, I remember," Bea said. "It was the only time he ever closed his doors for so long. I think he was out for two weeks. He had that black wreath on the door and that pretty note to the customers about her going home and the angels and such. It breaks my heart to think of it now."

I nodded. I sadly remembered that, too. "I think it's safe to say it was no jaded wife or her 'other man.'"

Aunt Astrid shook her head, agreeing with me. Then her eyes widened as they did when she had an idea. "He has children, right? A daughter, at least. Anyone being left out of a will or looking to inherit the business? People in desperate situations resort to desperate means."

"What about disgruntled employees?" Bea offered.

Suddenly, I slapped my hand to my forehead. "I hate to say this." I rubbed the back of my neck.

"What? You're hungry again?" Bea looked at me with a smirk.

"What? No." I bumped her with my elbow. "Darla."

Arch Nemesis

"What would Darla have to do with Marvin?" Aunt Astrid asked.

Darla Castellan was my arch-nemesis in high school. She had decided our sophomore year that her proverbial claws needed continual sharpening, and I was to be the instrument used to keep them pointy and dangerous.

Like a young Clark Kent, I had powers no one would let me use. Unlike Clark Kent, who could run and had super strength, I possessed the ability to afflict Darla with warts. I could have caused her to have a paralyzing fear of pencils, or I could have made the grass and trees pull and yank at her as she walked by. But I never did. Instead, I had to take her abuse.

Darla was wealthy and beautiful and spoiled rotten. The boys loved her, but most of the girls were scared of her wrath. After seeing how she treated me, they were too afraid to stand up to her.

As if that power weren't enough, she thought she could dive into Greenwood history and master the art of witchcraft, too. Her selfish actions resulted not only in the Brew-Ha-Ha going up in flames but also in the death of our previous baker, Ted. She didn't kill him outright, but she could have saved him if she'd had even a shred of conscience.

"Darla worked for Marvin back when she was in college," I said.

"But that was several years ago. What would she be mad at from then that she'd remember now? *And* seek revenge?" Bea asked.

"Well, first Darla got fired from that job. I had heard around the neighborhood that she wasn't just rude to customers, but that she had a real aversion to doing any kind of actual work. I mean, look at her." I raised my hands with my palms up. "Is it any wonder she married money?"

"Then divorced it," Bea said smugly.

"Then got half of everything and is looking for the next lucky Mr. Castellan," Aunt Astrid added.

"I also heard she was blackballed after that

because Marvin wasn't going to lie for her and give her any kind of reference," I said. "Plus, she's so dumb, half the town knew she had been working there, having seen her with their own eyes and experiencing her radiant personality. She wasn't going to get a job in this town anywhere." I was unable to contain my glee while repeating the story. I knew gossip was bad, but this gossip was the truth.

"Where did you hear all this?" Bea asked.

"From none other than Ruby Connors."

Both Bea's and Aunt Astrid's eyes got as wide as saucers.

Ruby Connors was Darla's lackey all through high school and still was. I thought Ruby liked the attention that trickled off of Darla and sometimes splashed on her. But if I got Ruby alone, she couldn't help herself. She'd spill the beans on her own mother if it made her the center of attention for a few seconds without the model-perfect Darla.

"Still." Aunt Astrid shook her head skeptically. "That was several years ago. She's moved on, don't you think?"

It was my turn to shake my head. "Have you ever known Darla to move on after someone did her wrong?" I folded my arms over my chest as if I had just cracked the case wide open.

"But this is magic, Cath. We got the book back from her. We watched you erase her memories and even helped put new ones in their place. You don't think that we missed something? That her memories somehow grew back and she's trying to hone her craft again, do you?" Bea asked nervously.

"I don't know." I shrugged. "But she's as logical a first step as anyone else at this point."

"If she is up to her old tricks again, she'll be covered in residual magic," Aunt Astrid said. "Based on the description you gave of the coroner's office, she wouldn't be able to shake that off of her for a couple of days. We just need to get a look at her to tell."

I shivered at the thought of being anywhere near that woman. "Yeah, okay. How are we going to do that? Heaven knows she would be suspicious if I suddenly showed up at her door."

"I know," Bea said. "I'll call her and tell her she's won a free lunch at the café. We pulled her business card from the bowl."

"We don't have a bowl of business cards," Aunt Astrid pointed out.

"Doesn't matter. She doesn't know that because she goes to the Night Owl Café. We can just say someone must have dropped it in for her. Whatever.

It'll get her there. She won't turn down a free lunch *and* an opportunity to gloat."

I nodded and smiled. "Nice one, cuz. I like your thinking. And I like how you're going to wait on her and do all the talking while I hang out in the kitchen until she leaves."

"Fine. Leave me to face the Gorgon alone," Bea joked then yawned loudly.

"It's late, girls. We need to get some rest. All of us. If it's Darla, we're going to have a heck of a mess on our hands. The better prepared we are, the better off we'll be. So rest up, and I'd suggest we all wear a protection spell tomorrow just in case."

We all agreed. Bea and I left Aunt Astrid's, and I walked Bea to her car.

"Hey, before you go, I have a question." I linked my arm through Bea's. "What did you say to Blake that got him to take you back to see the body? Did you put a spell on him or something?"

"Of course not." Bea smirked at me.

"Well, what did you do? Because had *I* asked, he would have had me on the ground, slapped in hand-cuffs, dragged to the backseat of the squad car, and on my way to the station before I could say hocus-pocus."

"That is because I can attract flies with sugar, and

you are still trying to do it with vinegar." She slipped her arm gently out of mine and quickly climbed behind the wheel of her car.

I gave her a blank stare. "Okay. Be sure to use some of that sugar on your favorite person, Darla. Yup! Lots and lots of sugar!" I yelled as her car pulled away.

I turned and started to walk in the direction of my house when I froze. For a second, I thought I had heard Treacle. I strained to listen and held my breath. I called to him in my mind then waited. Nothing.

Did I imagine it? Was it just wishful thinking? I don't know, but as I made my way home, I walked almost on tiptoe, breathing slowly and trying hard to hear past all the quiet.

Magic Residue

The next day, Bea called Darla to inform her she'd won the weekly business card drawing. In addition to a free gourmet lunch created by the new baker, Kevin, the drawing entitled her to a homemade dessert, an herbal tea infused with fresh fruit, and a small hot coffee the next time she came in.

"That means she's going to come in one more time after this." I wrinkled my nose.

"Afraid so," Bea said. "Unless, of course, we find her guilty of death by witchcraft, and then, well, justice will have to prevail."

"Now if that doesn't give me mixed emotions about this whole situation, I don't know what does." I put my hand on my hip. "When is she coming in?"

Just then, the front door jingled, and I instinctively looked up. There she was.

"Hi, Darla," Bea said in an overly sugary sweet tone. "Congratulations."

Pulling her long, black hair behind her and letting out a deep breath, Darla reciprocated with a quick smile that squinted her eyes into tiny slits for a split second then snapped back to her normal grimace.

She looked around the Brew-Ha-Ha. "I haven't seen the place since it was a smoldering mess. I didn't realize it, but the Night Owl has the most fantastic soups. I've been eating there at least once a week. I tell everyone I know they have to taste it to believe. Best food in town if you ask me."

I was about ready to tell her to drag her sorry behind back to the Night Owl, but I remembered Bea's reason for getting her to the café in the first place. I tried to peek in Bea's direction but couldn't tell if she had seen anything on Darla or not.

"Well, we really hope you enjoy your lunch," Bea said sweetly.

Darla jingled her bracelets, several gold, sparkly things that I'm sure cost a small fortune, and pushed them away from her watch with perfectly manicured nails. "Yes, well, I'm meeting with my accountant this afternoon, so if we could hurry things up, that would be great."

"Just give me a second to get it all together for you." Bea turned and swiveled around the counter and into the kitchen.

Letting out a deep sigh, Darla looked me up and down. Within a split second, I was transported back to my sophomore year in high school, feeling awkward and out of place. I had to remind myself that we were in my café, my family was right there, and Darla couldn't bully me like she used to. But still, old wounds ran deep.

"Um, Cath?"

I snapped out of my trance and turned toward the kitchen to see Bea peeking around the corner.

Aunt Astrid had taken her usual seat at the small table for two at the end of the counter. She was filling sugar holders, folding paper napkins, and watching Darla as inconspicuously as possible.

When I looked at Bea, she mouthed, *"It's not her."*

I nodded and bit my lower lip. I was glad Darla didn't have the telltale residue of magic spells on her since we knew from our last experience with her that she wasn't very capable. Magic requires patience and common sense. And if you're going to do it right, magic requires that you have a heart to guide your decisions. As far as I could tell, Darla didn't have a heart.

Aunt Astrid went back to filling the sugar holders and nodded slowly. I could tell she was thinking about what we should do next.

Darla looked around the café, and her eyes homed in on the only man sitting by himself. I'd seen him in the café before. He was a nice-looking guy in his early thirties, with light brown hair going gray at his temples, and an athletic build. He was just Darla's type—male.

Darla took a seat at the tiny table next to him. After crossing her long legs, only a few minutes passed before the man struck up a conversation with her.

Aunt Astrid watched discreetly with mild amusement. I wasn't as discreet and openly stared at Darla. Something inside of me hoped to see a sign of shiftiness or deceit on her face that might give her away. Maybe I could catch something Bea missed.

Unfortunately, all I saw was the same girl from high school who always got whatever she wanted. I don't know how long I stared at her, but she caught me and gave me a look, tilting her head with the attitude of a Hollywood prima donna.

I rolled my eyes and went back to wiping down the counter.

"You sure you got nothing?" I asked, turning my back to the counter and leaning against it. "Not a sliver, not a shred, nothing that we could use to lock her up for a couple of days?"

"Give me just a second." Bea quietly scooted past me with a fantastic-smelling veggie sandwich and a tall glass of our homemade iced tea with raspberries. She also handed Darla a fork and knife wrapped in a napkin, and I saw their fingers touch. When Bea turned around, she shook her head. "Other than a slight case of constipation, she's clean."

"Well, that's something." I felt a little satisfaction.

"Of course, after she eats my healthy, complementary lunch, that won't be a problem for her either." Bea frowned at me. "Sorry, Cath. I should have given her something with beans in it. I wasn't thinking."

"I know you would have, Bea. Thanks."

By early afternoon, I was busy helping Kevin in the back with inventory when Aunt Astrid called my name. "Cath, someone here to see you!"

Toffees

✦❀✦

As I came around the corner, I saw that Darla was still there. Her new friend had pulled up a chair and made himself comfortable at her table, leaning in to talk.

"Cath." I turned to see my best friend Min Park.

"Hey!" I suddenly felt happy and confident.

Min and I had met in high school and had been glued at the hip until we graduated. Min had recently moved back to Wonder Falls a retired millionaire, and I could honestly say nothing had changed in him. He was still the sweetest guy I'd ever known.

I gave him a big hug. "What brings you in here at this hour? Let me guess. It's the people." I jerked my head to the right, making Min turn toward Darla who was obviously trying her hardest to look as though she weren't paying attention to us.

Min's fortune never made a difference to me. Whether he'd come back rich or poor wasn't the issue. I was just thrilled he'd come back to Wonder Falls.

Darla, on the other hand, hated the fact he'd come back to town a multimillionaire. Not only was he the richest resident in ten counties, but he had no interest in Darla, and that was what bothered her the most.

His disinterest in her wasn't just because she was mean to me for sport or because of idle gossip or teenage teasing. Her affiliation with Ruby Connors was why Min would never have anything to do with Darla.

Ruby Connors's big brother tormented Min. One horrible moonlit night, Ruby's brother stuffed Min in a sack and dumped him in the river. It took some fancy maneuvering on my part and a deal with the Lady in the Lake to rescue him. He almost died that night. But that is a story for another time.

Darla turned to stare at me. I knew it was killing her that Min and I were still such good friends, and that he had heaps of money.

Of course, I liked Min before he made his

fortune. Rich or poor never made a difference to me, which was probably part of the reason Min and I were such good friends and the reason why Darla and I would probably always be mortal enemies.

The sweetest thing about his success was that without trying, Min had achieved the most divine retribution against the bullies he'd had to deal with. He was happy, healthy, and just happened to be rich.

"Can I get some of that chocolate you guys have? The little toffees?" In all the years I'd known Min, he'd never had a huge sweet tooth. A man after Bea's own heart, he liked fruit and maybe, if he were splurging, a little honey as sweetener. But he usually came in for green tea and not much else.

"Of course you can." I pulled out one of our delicate little bags with The Brew-Ha-Ha written in antique script across it. "But eat them slow. We won't be getting anymore of this quality for a while."

"Really? Why is that?" he asked.

Darla had shifted in her seat and was trying to hear what I was saying. I turned my back to her and slipped my arm through Min's to pull him down closer to me so I could talk semi-privately. "Marvin the chocolatier at Sweetie's is dead. Died of a heart attack just yesterday morning." I released Min's arm and folded the top of the little bag over then added a gold sticker to hold it shut.

"You're kidding," Min said in a hushed voice.

I shook my head as I handed him the candy. When he reached for his wallet, I waved my hand.

"On the house, as always. And no, I'm not kidding. You didn't hear anything about it?" I probed a little.

Min didn't know about my bewitching family history, and I preferred to keep it that way. If our friendship were to ever progress in a more intimate direction, I'd fess up, but at that moment, I was just your average woman asking about the latest town gossip.

"No. Nothing at all." He looked down at me with shock on his face. "I have been spending a lot of time at the nursing home. I haven't had a lot of time to even see my parents, let alone get the scoop on what's happening with the locals."

"You're right. You have been very busy. I haven't seen your bright face around here as much. Is everything going okay with the Wonder Falls Retirement Community? Are they liking their new Chairman of the Board?"

One of Min's goals when he returned to Wonder Falls was to give back to the community. He chose to start volunteering at the old folks' home. Maybe it was his Asian heritage that made him feel more indebted to the older members of our community since it was part of his tradition, or maybe it was just that he had a kind heart. Either way, he was helping, which was ultimately what he wanted to do.

"Oh, I think they are liking me fine." His cheeks reddened as he looked down at his shoes and smiled.

"Min? Are you…blushing?" I bumped him with my hip. "Something is up. Tell me now before I have to resort to violence."

Finally sitting on a stool at the counter, Min made himself comfortable and ordered tea. I hopped around the other side of the counter, propped my head up on my hands and waited.

"Her name is Amalia."

My jaw dropped. A girl?

"She's a nurse at the Home. She's been there for over two years but had worked the graveyard shift…"

"Not a good term to use in regard to the 'old folks' home.'" I used air quotes to emphasize my point. Any talk of graves, tombstones, or death should be avoided at all cost for fear of bad jokes ensuing.

"Right?" Min chuckled a little. "When her

schedule changed due to one of our older nurses retiring, I got the chance to meet her."

I smiled. "I see." Was I happy about this? I don't know. It was the first time Min had ever mentioned a girl—no, a nurse. A woman. It was the first time he'd ever mentioned a woman to me. I had to admit I was feeling a little weird.

"You'd like her, Cath. I know you would."

"I'm...sure that I would, Min. I'm really happy for you. You'll have to bring her into the café sometime."

Just then, Darla stood, making a spectacle of herself by flipping her hair and giggling at something her new boy toy had said. He was already grabbing her purse to carry for her, and they both scooted out of the café. How did she train them so fast?

"She didn't even say if she liked the meal," Aunt Astrid scoffed, shaking her head in disgust as she finished the last of her napkin folding.

"Well, she did everything but lick the plate clean," Bea said, holding up the plate, which looked as if no food had even been served on it. "She didn't stay for her dessert."

"She couldn't, remember? She had a very important meeting with her accountant," I said, not holding back the sarcasm.

"It's about time someone made her handle her own finances. We all know she's been mooching off these poor men long enough." Aunt Astrid slowly stood and stretched her bones. The lunch rush was over.

"She'll be back, you know, to collect on that. It's just an excuse for her to come in and do a little snooping. She's so obvious." I didn't try to hide my feelings, yet I felt a pinch of irony since we lured her there to do the exact same thing.

"Your feelings for her haven't changed," Min said sympathetically.

"It would take divine intervention to make me even consider changing my opinion of Darla. Sometimes, high school brings out the jerk in people, but when they remain that way years later, then you know the problem is them. If I never saw her again, it would be too soon."

Min patted my hand. "She's like that because she's jealous of you, you know."

"Of course she is. I have this good-looking guy that I call my best friend. Who could blame her?"

Min smiled broadly and puffed out his chest. "So, you started to tell me about the chocolatier before. Tell me what happened." He cupped his hand under his chin and leaned forward. I scooted a little closer, and it felt as though we were back in high school discussing our secrets and stories at one of the lunch tables.

I never would have imagined that at any time our secrets and stories would involve a dead chocolatier...and a new girlfriend. I certainly wasn't prepared for there to be a connection between the two.

Cat Attack

❧❦❧

Another day had gone by without a word from Treacle. I was beside myself with worry and couldn't relax. Even when I was sitting, my nerves were stretching and pulling inside of my skin.

Finally, I decided I couldn't just sit around and wait for him anymore. I had to go out on my own and see if I could find a furry associate of his who could give me a tip or point me in a new direction.

The funny thing about being able to talk to cats is that I have to alter my mind to think like they do. It was easier than learning Chinese but harder than talking to yourself inside your own head.

Thinking like Treacle was going to take me in a myriad of directions I had never even imagined. Most cats loved to prowl at night, so I waited until the sun went down. Cats were connected to the supernatural, so they left a sort of footprint when they were out stalking about. It was how they could find their way back home so easily.

Unlike dogs that got lost and couldn't find their way back home, cats left a very light trail of energetic breadcrumbs they could pick up on. Even the smallest traces could linger for a long while, especially if it hadn't rained. And lucky for me, it hadn't.

With hope in my heart and tears in my eyes, I began my search. A small thread of Treacle's energy caught my attention, and I followed its glowing color from my house, through the streets, through a park, until finally it disappeared near the industrial area of Wonder Falls.

Deep in the industrial neighborhood was a building Aunt Astrid and I had broken into not long ago. At that time, the place housed a demon of sorts. The building was important because a feline had been there who had remembered Treacle. That puss even had a concrete opinion of me, so if I could find him, he might be helpful.

But I was having trouble finding anything that slinked on four legs. Usually, they sensed me as if I were one of them. They would come to inspect who was in their neighborhood. I got very nervous all of a sudden. Where had they all gone?

I continued at my casual pace. A few people were sitting on their stoops or hanging around on the corners, and they paid no attention to me.

I wasn't drawing attention to myself, and I had conjured up a camouflage spell before I left. I wasn't totally invisible, but I took on the appearance of what the gazer expected to see. In one instance, I might look like an old lady, and in another instance, I was just a young man making his way home. But the cats could see me as I was if any of them peeked out from their hiding places.

Finally, after a few more blocks, I caught sight of a calico peering from behind a dumpster. Her ears were flat back as she stared at me, her eyes glinting pale yellow against the darkness.

You look scared down there. I'm not going to hurt you, I said in my mind. I was speaking slow and clear, but the cat looked at me as if I were a junkyard dog. *I just want to ask you…*

The cat let out a hiss and darted off. She didn't say a word, but I could tell she was terrified of something. Whatever it was must have looked or acted like me… like a person. My blood was beginning to boil as I thought of someone terrorizing these cats.

Another black-and-white tuxedo cat slunk along the ledge of an old, run-down apartment building. A television light glowed through one of the apartment windows.

"Hey! You look like you see a lot of things going on around here," I called to the cat, again making my thoughts clear and calm. *"I was wondering…"*

In a split second, the cat arched its back, its fur stiffened, and it gave me a deep, guttural growl. My eyebrows shot up to my hairline. This had never happened before. Never.

As I watched the cat slink back underneath a raised window and into the apartment with the glowing television, I stopped for a moment to think.

During the days when witches and suspected witches were being burned at the stake, family stories and legends always mentioned how cats seemed to be aware before anyone else. In their simple minds, they knew a storm was coming, and they took shelter. Was that what was happening? Was a storm coming?

I kept walking. My camouflage spell was holding up, and I was weaving in and out of the neighborhoods with very little attention being paid to me.

Then I saw a familiar face. A large gray four-legged beastie glared at me the same as he'd done the last time I was in this part of town.

He was perched on a tall stack of skids at an alley entrance. I would never forget that cat's face, with his scarred mug and dirty, gray fur. He knew Treacle and didn't like him. He obviously picked up Treacle's scent on me and decided he didn't like me either.

"I know you," I said to him. He watched me with wild, wide eyes. *"You told me I didn't belong in this neighborhood and neither did the black cat I took care of. Do you remember?"* I stood perfectly still. I could see the muscles rippling underneath his fur as they tensed. *"I'm not going to hurt you. I was just wondering if you saw that black cat of mine. You know the one."*

He still didn't respond.

"What is wrong with all of you?" I mumbled out loud.

Finally, the big alley cat stood up. His fur was on edge, and his back arched as his unblinking eyes bore into mine. *"I've seen that one. Five nights ago."*

"Five nights ago? Where did he go?" I pointed up and down the street. *"What direction?"*

"He was lost in his mind. He walked in circles and mumbled and made his way through the buildings. He wouldn't fight. Couldn't fight and rushed past all of us. Something has him. He won't be back."

Tears filled my eyes. *"What? What has him? What are you talking about?"*

"There is a badness here. It's here! And it'll get you, too! You talking humans can't be trusted."

"Why would you say that? Wait." His words struck me. *"What other human is talking to you?"*

Call me territorial, but as far as I knew, being able to communicate with cats was a rare and special gift. If someone else had that same talent, I sure the heck wanted to know who it was and why, since that person had come to town, all the cats were more high-strung than ever before.

Like the crack of a whip, the cat leapt at me. His claws were out, and one sharp nail gouged my neck, leaving a long trail of torn skin that instantly began to bleed in a thin line. He pushed off my body and bound down the street, slinking underneath a parked car and into the shadows.

"What in the world?" I said out loud. I was crying openly. I had never had a cat attack me. Dogs, bats, even a raccoon may have tried to take a swipe at me before but never a cat.

The feline's words were of no comfort either. Treacle was in that neighborhood five days ago? He walked in circles? The only thing that came to mind was a word I didn't want to say. A horror worse than any other talking human for my poor, beautiful cat, and if it were true, it would be all my fault.

I took a few steps, not knowing what direction to go. I thought back to the last time I saw Treacle and wished I could go back to that moment. If I would have kept him in the house, maybe he wouldn't be lost and possibly hurt. I was used to letting him go and picking him up at the animal shelter or seeing him weave in through the back door of the café. I had taken him for granted.

Rabies.

No, I wasn't ready to say the word or even think it. That horrible disease eats an animal up slowly and painfully from the inside, starting with its mind. Hadn't Treacle had his shots? I know I'd gotten them for him at the shelter. I know I had.

Hadn't I?

Rabies. No, there had to be another explanation. Treacle would have come home if he'd been attacked that badly. I would have seen a wound or a bite or something. No, something more sinister was at play.

I was near hysterics. Treacle may not have had rabies, but something was hurting him. Something was keeping him from me, and I needed to find out what it was and make sure it never harmed him or any other cat again.

My heart was broken, and I felt very tired. It was as though a weight had been added to my shoulders and ankles. I needed to get home so I could rest and figure out what to do next.

That big alley cat may not have been telling the truth. But that thought was no comfort.

As I made my way back home, I recalled taking Treacle to the vet for his shots. Wonder Falls had a lot of bats, raccoons, squirrels, and other things that could have gotten a hold of him at any time. I didn't take chances because I knew how much he loved to roam.

But even if he didn't have rabies, what if he had some other disease? What if he had gotten into a fight with something bigger and meaner than he was? What if he was hurt and wondering where I was? I felt my heart crack into pieces. I had to find him, no matter what.

Enchantment Spell

꽃

The next day, I showed up at the Brew-Ha-Ha half an hour before we opened, and I must have looked a dozen shades of pitiful.

"Cath? What's the matter?" Bea asked, her eyes wide with concern. "Mom! It's Cath!" She poured me a glass of water as I took a seat at the counter.

"I'm okay. I just didn't get much sleep last night."

"Cath, Bea, what's the matter?" My aunt came from the kitchen where she probably had been helping Kevin. She wiped her hands on her apron, and her look of annoyance was quickly replaced with concern. "My heaven's, Cath. What happened?"

I swallowed hard. "Treacle hasn't come back."

Both women looked at each other then back at me. "I went out last night looking for him. I didn't find him. None of the cats were talking. They're terrified of something. And one of them… " I took a drink of water to clear my throat and tried to hold back the tears. "One of them managed to tell me they saw him, and he was not acting right. He said Treacle was lost in his mind and mumbling. But that was five days ago. Where could he be?" I lost my composure and began crying like a baby.

Losing my parents was sad, and I missed them terribly. But a pet was different. Most people thought pets relied on us to take care of and protect them. I thought we relied on our pets to protect our hearts. The world could be a scary and lonely place. The animals we kept prevented that world from becoming too much to bear.

"Has Marshmallow been acting any differently?" Bea asked her mother. "Peanut Butter is still so young that I can't tell when he is onto something or when he's just chasing a shadow."

Aunt Astrid thought for a moment then shook her head. "But you have to remember that my house, like yours, is protected with an enchantment spell. Our cats don't leave the houses. But your cat is a roamer, Cath, and only the threshold spell will protect him if he's inside the house." Aunt Astrid made sure we all had some kind of protection on our homes. "Plus, Treacle has been a roamer since he was a kitten. There is nothing you could have done to keep him inside if he wanted to go outside. You know that."

I nodded and wiped my nose with a napkin.

Aunt Astrid pursed her eyebrows and stared at the floor. She nodded and then shook her head as if responding to someone else. She mumbled a few words under her breath before looking up at Bea and me. "I think this has something to do with Marvin."

I cleared my throat noisily. "What? Why do you think that?"

Aunt Astrid walked around the counter and sat on the stool next to me. She folded her hands on the counter and continued to stare down. It looked as though she was studying the grains of the dark wood.

"We have some pretty good proof that this witch is not very good at what she does. She or he likes to call themselves a witch more than they care to know the history, the theories, the proper procedures. They like the image and care not for the substance."

"What does that have to do with Treacle?" Bea asked.

"He's a black cat. Black cats are the most magical. I think he's hiding from this wanna-be witch. If what you're saying about all the other cats is true, he may be hiding, too."

"But what about what the gray alley cat said about him not being right in the head and stuff?" I hoped Aunt Astrid might have an answer to dowse the flames of nervousness in my belly.

"His solid black coat makes him very attractive to anyone dabbling in the occult. If they are dabbling and doing it all wrong, as we think this witch is, Treacle could be getting hit the hardest."

"That is, if he isn't…"

Bea reached across the counter and squeezed my hands. She had wet eyes, too. "Don't say it, Cath. Just don't. Treacle might be in bad shape, but he's still alive. That gray kitty would have told you otherwise, especially since he made it clear he didn't like you very much."

Someone suddenly knocked on the glass door. All of us looked to see the faces of a couple of regulars and some new patrons waiting for us to open the café.

"Oh, geez!" Aunt Astrid yipped, hopping off the

stool and running to the door. "Sorry, folks! Just a little family business to tend to. Come on in. Glad you're here. Free fortune-telling today for the first five customers. That will make things better, no?"

I hopped off the stool and hurried behind the counter to help Bea. It was a beautiful morning. I couldn't help but think it was the calm before the storm. My body moved mechanically as I served our regulars and smiled, saying "good morning" and "have a nice day." My mind was in a million places at once, yet I couldn't cling to a single thought. It was frustrating.

"I'll be right back," I said to Bea. She patted my shoulder and nodded. I walked to the ladies' room at the back of the café, needing a minute to myself. I ran my hands under the cold water and looked in the mirror. My eyes were red and tired. I'd been up all night, and it was starting to catch up with me. Just as I decided to ask for a personal day, I heard a quiet knock on the door.

"I'll be out in a second," I called through the door.

"Honey, Min is here," Aunt Astrid said politely.

"Oh, okay."

"He's, uh… not alone."

I dried my hands on my pants and opened the door. "Really?"

She nodded and walked back to the front of the café. I smoothed my hair back and imagined who Min was with. It had to be a girl, or Aunt Astrid wouldn't have said anything. Of course, today had to be the day I met Min's new girlfriend.

A Lead

✿❀✿

Truth be told, I was thankful for the distraction. After spending almost the entire night worrying about Treacle, I needed something else to focus on.

I walked around the kitchen to the front of the café and saw Min standing next to a petite young lady. She had curly, auburn hair, wide eyes, and freckles over the bridge of her nose. Min was talking with Bea, and the young lady was also contributing to the conversation, laughing and nodding at whatever Bea was saying.

Aunt Astrid tugged on my sleeve from her regular seat. "You all right?"

"I'll be fine. I know I'll find Treacle. He's around somewhere and…"

"I meant about this." She jerked her chin in Min's direction.

"What? Oh my gosh." I hoped my reply was convincing. "Of course. Are you serious?"

Aunt Astrid's right eyebrow arched, and she gave me a sideways look.

I rolled my eyes at her and walked up to Min with my shoulders back and my chin held high.

When he turned and saw me, he smiled. "Cath!" he stooped down to give me a hug.

I hugged him back, and for a moment, I felt a little superior to the woman. I didn't want to feel that way, but it crept up inside me like an aggressive vine that wrapped itself around my heart.

For years, it had been Min and me against the world. When he left to make his fortune, I didn't worry about what he was doing or who he was with, and when he came back, we picked up right where we left off. You can only do that with a rare friend. I had been spoiled.

For so long, Min had been my shoulder to cry on, my pillar of strength, my confidant. But he'd found a cute woman who was going to share her secrets and her dreams with him and, who knew, maybe even more than that.

Min pulled away first, and I followed suit. I didn't want to come across as one of those women who were clingy and needy, even if all I wanted to do was cling to Min because I needed his help to find Treacle. I stood back and waited for the bomb of disappointment and annoyance to go off between his girlfriend and me.

"Cath, this is Amalia. Amalia, this is my best friend in the whole world, Cath Greenstone," Min said.

The woman walked around the table and gave me a gentle, heartfelt hug. Some people may have thought it was a little forward to hug someone upon first meeting them, but with the way I was feeling at the moment, I really appreciated it.

"I am so glad to meet you," she said in a clear and kind voice. "Min has told me so much about you that I feel like I've known you my whole life." She pulled back and smiled pleasantly.

"Don't believe him. He likes to elaborate and lie," I said, making Amalia laugh. "Please, guys, have a seat. Let me get you something to drink. Coffee, tea, lemonade or a water or…"

"I'd love a tea," Amalia said. "I just got off work and don't want anything too strong to keep me up. I'll need a nap for sure."

"I'll get them," Min offered. "You ladies can talk behind my back for a few minutes."

I looked awkwardly at Amalia, who didn't seem to be uncomfortable or nervous at all.

"It must have been a full moon or something last night because several of the residents had me running my tail off from the minute I got there to when I checked out this morning." Amalia rolled her eyes. "First, Mr. Lessing said he heard scratching on the walls. The residents are allowed to have small pets, and Mr. Lucio's cat got out of his room and was finally cornered in the recreational center after knocking over half a dozen potted plants. Mrs. Toon said there was a person outside digging at the corner of the building. The best one was Mr. Cavanaugh who said he needed a sponge bath because Marilyn Monroe was planning on paying him a visit."

I smiled, and a little laugh rattled out of my chest.

"If Mr. Cavanaugh had his way, he'd have a sponge bath every hour."

I felt my heart get a little lighter. "That's funny."

"Don't get me wrong. I love working at the Home. The job can be hard at times, but I love the stories around all the residents. Sometimes, one or two of them just decide they want to cause a little drama. It's like high school."

She was charming. I hated to admit it, but I felt a possible friendship tugging at my thoughts. The corners of my mouth would not stay down. I smiled, and it felt good.

"I'm sorry I'm so talky." She patted my hand quickly. "I get this way when I'm tired."

"Would you like a chamomile tea? My cousin adds a little lavender-infused honey, and even though I'm not a tea drinker, I have to say it's really soothing."

Amalia stared at me with her mouth open. "That sounds like heaven. Yes. Yes, I would like that. Thank you. Please."

I laughed again and waved for Bea to make her special tea for Amalia. We chatted a little more until Min sat down with us. Then I really got an earful.

"So the man who made those delicious toffees passed away? Min was telling me about it." Amalia wrapped her hands around the sides of her warm mug of tea. I was glad she wasn't hanging on Min. They sat close to each other, but they weren't all touchy-feely like new couples sometimes were.

"Yeah. It was a heart attack, we heard," I said.

"That was Marvin Clegg, right?" Amalia asked, squinting her eyes a little.

"Yeah, it was," I said.

"That's really bizarre because just a few weeks ago, I'd say maybe two weeks ago, his daughter, Brit Clegg, had come in inquiring about a place for him at the home."

My heart leapt. "Really. Gosh, that's weird. Was she nice?"

Amalia took a sip of her tea and rolled her eyes. "Oh my gosh. This *is* soothing. Holy moly. Yes, she was very nice. But now that you mention it…"

I held my breath and leaned in.

"She was a little vague about some of the questions we routinely ask, and then she had some strange questions for us." She took another sip. "I remember wondering what kind of daughter asks if female visitors other than her can come to her father's room and stay overnight?"

"That is weird," I said. "What else did she say?"

"Well, she asked if there were cameras, and she asked if her father could burn candles and incense in his room."

"Well, maybe she was just concerned with security, and maybe her dad liked incense. My late Uncle Karl had a dog that died, and he kept a picture of it with a little votive candle burning all the time. Maybe he had something like that going on. His wife did pass away several years ago."

"Maybe." Amalia shrugged and took another sip of her tea. "The weirdest thing was that she wanted to know all these things but said her father didn't know she was inquiring. She said she didn't know when he'd be ready to move in, just that it would be soon."

"And now he's dead," I said thoughtfully.

"I know. It's so sad. If only she could have gotten him in there sooner, he'd have had medical attention as soon as it happened. He might still be alive today."

Not with an exploded heart, I thought. "Was his daughter living here?"

"Yeah, that was another strange thing. When I asked her for her home address and a phone number where we could contact her, she gave the address to a rental located in, well, not a very good part of town. Do you know where all those warehouses and random mills are located? Apparently she's living over there. Wishing Well Court trailer park. Frankly, I wasn't sure how she was going to pay for her father's room, but many people find ways when they need to."

I thought of my adventure to find Treacle. His trail had gone cold just as I was roaming through that area. Whatever was there was affecting the cats, too. This was the biggest break I could have hoped for.

Amalia let out a big yawn. "I'm so sorry to be yawning. It isn't the company, really, but I am beat. I think it's your cousin's tea. It's like sipping a down pillow and comforter."

Min and I laughed. "I better take you home," Min said. "Tonight, we're going to the Music Box to catch *Casablanca* on the big screen. Cath, do you want to come with us?"

"Say yes," Amalia said. "You'll have fun. I've seen that movie at least a dozen times, and I just can't see it enough. When the French start singing their national anthem over the Germans'... I get goose bumps talking about it."

I would have loved to go, but the wheels in my head were spinning.

"You know, thank you so much for inviting me, but I can't. I've got plans with my aunt and Bea that have to do with family stuff. Boring but necessary, you know."

"I do." She yawned again.

"Let's make plans to do something together

soon," Min said, beaming with a happiness I knew was because Amalia and I had hit it off.

I smiled back. I couldn't tell him, but meeting Amalia was more wonderful than he could ever know. Not only had she given us a lead on the real cause of Marvin's death, but she'd also given us a lead suspect. And quite possibly, she may have given me a tip to where Treacle might be. If there was a witch in that area, she might have *my* black cat.

Even after the terrible night I'd had, I felt rejuvenated and couldn't wait to tell Bea and Aunt Astrid what I'd found out. All I needed was Brit Clegg's address.

After I told them, we agreed not to talk about our new discovery at work. Once the doors were locked and the CLOSED sign hung in the door, we met at Aunt Astrid's for a nightcap.

Wishing Well

✿

"The Wishing Well Trailer Park is huge, and it goes way back into the woods," Bea said. "Those trailers are secluded for a reason. It's not exactly the kind of place you want to go around asking questions."

"Why would Marvin's daughter be staying there when he had a successful business and a nice house in an affluent part of town?" Aunt Astrid asked. "That doesn't make any sense."

"Maybe they didn't get along," I said. Neither my aunt nor Bea said anything. "I'm going to go and do some looking around." I felt the strong gust of a second wind coming over my tired body.

Bea put her hands on her hips. "Cath, Wishing Well isn't a safe place. You shouldn't go by yourself.

You shouldn't go at all. Look, if we wait until tomorrow after we've slept on it, we'll be better prepared to come up with a plan. But for you to just go snooping around is crazy. Besides, you don't know what Marvin's daughter looks like, and there are hundreds of trailers in there. What are you going to do, knock on their doors?"

"No, I'm not going to knock on their doors. I just want to get a look at things. See what we're dealing with. Maybe see if I can pick up a vibe or two."

Aunt Astrid took my hands in hers across the book-covered dining room table and closed her eyes. "It's no use, Bea. You know how your cousin is once she gets a bee in her bonnet." Astrid mumbled a few words I could barely make out, and I knew she was putting a protection spell over me. Letting go of my hands, she gave me a wink.

"You're not going alone," I heard a familiar voice say. *"I'm going with you."* It was Marshmallow. She rubbed her head against my calf.

I looked down at her and smiled. *"Thank you, but whatever is going on doesn't seem to be cat-friendly. I couldn't bear it if something happened to you* and *Treacle."*

"That is exactly why you're taking me," she insisted. A curt meow was all Aunt Astrid and Bea heard. *"You're taking me with you."* She laid her paws on my

foot, and I felt the tiny prick of her claws starting to come out.

Letting out a deep sigh, I interrupted Bea and Aunt Astrid, who were still talking about the weird alignment of the facts we had so far. "It seems I won't be going alone after all." Marshmallow jumped up on the table.

Just then, Peanut Butter scurried around the corner in a panic. He was still young compared to Treacle and Marshmallow. He loved to visit Marshmallow when Bea brought her along. Peanut Butter would stalk, pounce, swat, and dart from room to room with just the slightest, if any, provocation. Marshmallow would watch him with dreamy and disinterested eyes.

"*You can't go,*" Peanut Butter cried. "*Who'll take care of me?*"

Marshmallow peered over the table and meowed back. "*I have to. We have to find Treacle. I can help. He'd do it for us.*"

"*Then I'm going with you,*" Peanut Butter said in almost a hiss.

"*No,*" I said firmly in my mind. "*You are too young. I don't like the idea of taking Marshmallow. I'm not taking you along, too.*"

"*I'll be all alone,*" Peanut Butter cried sadly.

"I'll be back. With Treacle."

"Promise?"

Marshmallow looked at me. She was acting brave, but I could see fear in her eyes. She was a house cat. Rarely did she go outdoors unless a bird, mouse, or cricket was within a few feet of the door.

"I promise," I said.

Marshmallow purred and rubbed her head under my hand.

"It looks like I'll have this furry companion to help me," I said out loud.

"Oh no, Cath, I don't think so," Aunt Astrid said, scratching Marshmallow behind the ears. Then Marshmallow did something I'd never seen her do before—she swatted Aunt Astrid's hand away and bared her teeth. She didn't hiss, and I don't know if her claws were out, but Marshmallow let her mistress know she meant business.

"Sorry, Mom. Looks like you don't have much of a say in it," Bea said, her eyes wide with surprise.

"I promise we'll be careful," I said. "I won't let her out of my sight." But in the back of my mind, I was worried. I remembered how all the other cats behaved near that part of town. I also knew Marshmallow wasn't like Treacle. She didn't have experience roaming the streets, slipping along inside shadows, or making quick decisions to get away from danger. Still, she insisted, and she'd never asked to help before. Even though she loved her human family, the love of her lifelong feline friend was entirely different. She wasn't going to leave Treacle out there if she could help it.

I placed her gently in her travel box, loaded her into my car, and headed to the Wishing Well Trailer Park. I left Aunt Astrid's house feeling as though I were about to solve the mystery in a matter of hours. I'd have proof, a motive, and be able to tip off Jake and Blake in an anonymous phone call, giving them credit for arresting the woman who killed Marvin... his own daughter. The thought of it made me sad.

I'd give anything to see my parents again, and Marvin's daughter was so selfish that she thought her father's life was something to be thrown away like a toy she no longer had use for. On top of everything else, she may have kidnapped Treacle, thinking a black cat would improve her half-baked attempts at witchcraft. Nothing was going to stop me from finding her trailer even if I had to knock on every door.

Finding Treacle

✿

The sign for the Wishing Well Trailer Park was an old, faded piece of plywood cut into the shape of a wishing well. The peeling red letters appeared to have been partially scratched off so if you looked at the sign a certain way, the only defined letters were the "h," "ell," and Trailer Park.

I ignored the chill running up my spine as I drove past the entrance to the Wishing Well in search of someplace to park where no one would notice us. I saw a used car lot about a quarter of a mile down the road and an office building that looked like it had once been a Pizza Hut.

I decided to park in the used car lot. Thankfully, the cars in the lot looked a lot like mine. They were old, a little rusty, and not very glamorous. The only difference was that my car didn't have the $2500 OBO or 87,000 miles written in soap on the windows. But I didn't plan on staying around long enough for anyone to notice my car.

"*You doing okay?*" I asked Marshmallow. She didn't purr as I lifted her from her box. I felt her nails instinctively come out when I held her to my chest.

"*I'm okay,*" she said quietly in her head.

"*Do you want to walk, or should I carry you?*"

"*I'll walk. It's all right.*"

Gently, I set her down. For a moment, she stood perfectly still. Her body was low to the ground as she looked around, and for a moment, I thought she was going to bolt. "*There is something here, but it isn't what you think it is. I can feel it.*" She stared into the dark woods separating the trailer park from the used car lot.

"*What do you see?*" I asked, looking into the darkness.

"*I see fear.*"

As if shaking like a leaf and second-guessing my idea to visit the trailer park weren't bad enough, my companion then said all she could see was fear. I didn't even want to know what that looked like.

Marshmallow walked ahead of me. I knew if she

heard anything, she'd stop, yet I held my breath and listened for any unusual sounds—footsteps, groaning, weird whispers, and anything else I'd seen in a horror movie. I desperately hoped I didn't hear the rev of a chainsaw.

Okay, I was being silly. Thankfully, the ground was even. It wasn't full of dips and mounds, and there weren't tons of fallen trees and sticker bushes. Most of the trees were thin and relatively young by tree standards. I grabbed onto them as I walked. The darkness was thick, and I used the trees to maintain my balance. Touching nature always grounded me. Trees were real. I didn't feel magic or spells yet.

After a few more paces, Marshmallow and I saw a faint, green-tinted fluorescent light in the distance. Squinting, I could see a few trailers in its weakly illuminated circle.

"We're almost there," I said. Marshmallow gave me a quiet meow as a response.

I looked behind us and could no longer see the lights of the used car dealership. It was as if the whole world had dropped into some black place. If a tree fell in the woods, and no one was around, did it make noise? If you couldn't see the lights, was the dealership still there? If Marshmallow and I had to run back, would we eventually see the lights, or would we keep running and running in darkness?

I shook my head and focused on the lights before us. The trailers were nothing like the trailers at the front of the Wishing Well that faced the road. Those trailers had roots in a way. The people who lived in the front trailers had flowerbeds and even cement stairs leading up to their homes. I'd seen a tool shed or two and a few gazing balls. Statues of St. Francis, wind chimes, and sun catchers made the place look homey and attractive. A person driving by might think the homes didn't fit the stereotype of a trailer park. They looked clean, pretty, and proper. But when someone got to the back of the park where we were, he would see where reality lived.

Three trailers were huddled together under the sickly green lights. The trailers looked like members of the same gang, all of them beat up with dents and scratches. Two of the three trailers were most likely breaking the rules as they were supported by cinder blocks and what looked like plastic milk crates. Lit up from the inside, the windows displayed either dirty curtains drawn tightly shut, a trash bag, or thick towels preventing anyone from seeing in or out.

"This isn't where we want to be," Marshmallow said,

stopping in front of me. She raised her head, her whiskers twitching wildly, then crouched back down on her belly. *"But we aren't far. Something is up ahead."*

I looked where Marshmallow was looking. More trailers were lit by sickly green light. The lampposts were in just as bad a shape as the rest were.

Staying within the safety and confines of the trees, we skirted along the perimeter. The pitiful light from the trailer park cast menacing shadows all around us, but I was able to see, which made me calmer. It was a big park, and I began to think it was a bad idea to go snooping around.

But this wasn't really snooping, right? I wasn't peeking in windows or listening to conversations. That was snooping. I was just... exploring, trying to map out the lay of the land so I could snoop around later.

"There. Up ahead. Do you see that glow?" Marshallow asked.

I looked and squinted but saw nothing.

"It's coming from the middle of that row," Marshmallow said. *"We've got to go in there."*

I looked around, listening and scanning the shadows for any kind of movement, any hint that someone was watching us. But there was nothing.

"Stick to the shadows, and lead the way," I said,

watching Marshmallow morph from the lounging butterball of purring fur to a svelte predator on a mission.

We quietly and carefully slunk along the sides of the trailers, moving in between generators and storage pods until we got to where Marshmallow had seen the glow. I saw no glow. I only saw a dark trailer. It wasn't menacing like the three at the ass-end of the park, but it wasn't a showpiece like the ones at the entrance either.

It was simple—a white trailer, no wind chimes, no decorations on the lawn, wooden steps leading to the entrance. As I stood in the shadows, I realized I was starting to feel ill, as if something I had eaten was fussing deep in my gut. I swallowed hard and tried to shove it away.

"That's the house that's glowing?" I managed to say to Marshmallow but got no response. I assumed she was busy studying the terrain. Perhaps something else had caught her eye. I took a step closer to the trailer and again felt a wave of nausea settle over me. My skin was becoming cold and hot at the same time. I shivered, but I was also sweating. I couldn't imagine what I could have eaten that would hit me like that.

After a few deep breaths, I began to feel better. I

took a few steps closer to the plain, little trailer in the middle of the park.

A bunch of mason jars set on the steps leading to the front door. As I looked closer, I could see they had something in them. The jars held a yellow liquid and some odds and ends I couldn't make out. I counted eight jars on the steps, and to my surprise, they were in the windows, too.

I tried to inch a little closer but stopped cold. I gripped the side of the trailer behind which Marsh-mallow and I were hiding. *"Something is wrong with me,"* I said in my mind but still got no response. *"Marshmallow, what are you…"*

She was staring straight at me. We couldn't communicate. She couldn't hear me, and I couldn't hear her, yet we were right next to each other.

This wasn't right. My stomach was doing flips, and I was beginning to shake. Goose bumps had risen all over my arms and shoulders. I was about to scoop up the cat and head back to the woods when I stopped and held my breath.

Headlights. And they were coming this way. I flattened myself against the aluminum siding and tried to shrink into the shadows. If the car turned right, its lights would flash across us, and we'd be seen. If it turned left, we'd be okay. Closer and closer it came. Just then, lights popped on in the trailer, and I saw a familiar face in the window.

"Treacle!" I said in a hushed, sickly voice. Could he see us? Did he know we were there? I tried calling to him in my mind, but everything bounced back to me. What was going on?

Thankfully, the approaching car veered to the left and pulled into the gravel driveway of our plain, little trailer. A short woman, who I guessed to be in her early twenties, stepped out from the driver's side.

She wore jeans and a baggy shirt and carried a grocery bag. Gingerly, she stepped around the jars on her steps. Then she bent down and removed something from the threshold of her door. Rattling her keys, she unlocked the door, stepped inside, sprinkled something over the top step, replaced whatever had been in front of her door, then shut it quietly. From where we were, we heard several locks slip into place.

I wouldn't be able to kick in the door to get my cat. Even if I wanted to, I was in no condition to do it. My stomach was rolling up and over itself, and as I took a step closer to see what she had put in front of the door, I almost lost my balance.

It's a broom. A broom?

I noticed a gap in the curtain by the tiny window next to the door. I squinted and tried to see in, inching my way closer and closer to the front steps. I tried to see what was in the jars, too. A tiny light outside the door helped me to see.

Looking into the jars, I saw what appeared to be hair. It was repulsive. I knew I was too close and at any minute, I was sure I'd throw up, alerting not just the cat thief but the neighboring trailers as well. Finally, I couldn't take it anymore. With Marshmallow in my arms, I trudged back toward the trees. With every step, I started to feel better.

"Cath! Cath!" Marshmallow was screaming, clinging to my shirt. *"Why won't you answer me? I'm right here!"*

"Marshmallow! I couldn't hear you. Calm down. I can hear you now. Something was happening at that trailer."

"Did you see him? She has him! That person has…"

"Treacle. Yes. I saw him."

"Oh, how are we going to get him back?"

"I don't know. There's something going on at that place, but it wasn't a spell. At least, it wasn't any spell I've ever experienced. We've got to get Aunt Astrid and Bea. Maybe it's just something that affects me, you know, because Treacle is my cat. Maybe that's why I was getting sick. I don't know. But we need reinforcements for sure."

"Take me home. I don't want to be out here anymore." Marshmallow sounded pitiful. I snuggled her to me as we slowly made our way back to the used car lot and my car.

"You found Treacle, Marsh. I don't know what you saw that was glowing, but you saw it. I'd still be roaming around in there lost if it weren't for you. And Treacle is there."

"We have to come back to get him."

"Yes, we do."

"But how?"

I shook my head. The lights over the Pizza Hut-looking building guided us back.

"I don't know." I lowered Marshmallow back into her travel box. Before I even started the car, the cat was asleep. I wish I could do that.

That night, I tossed and turned. How was I going to get my cat back if the spell around that trailer made me feel like I had eaten a pail of dirt?

Witches' Vials

✤

"Jars of liquid and hair? Oh, dear." Aunt Astrid looked off in the distance.

Bea poured some of her strong Oolong tea into the tiny flowered cup setting in front of me.

I waved my hand. "Even after getting a couple hours sleep last night, I don't think I can keep anything down. There is still a twinge of sour that I just don't want to tempt."

Aunt Astrid's house was almost directly centered between my house and Bea's house. Jake always worked odd hours, so he was pretty understanding that we were always together.

I wrapped my arms around my stomach and sat

very still in my aunt's straight-backed dining room chair, trying desperately not to look at the Dutch apple pie she had within arm's reach.

"That poor girl," Aunt Astrid mumbled.

I didn't have to speak. Bea read my mind. "Poor girl? She stole Treacle. She killed her father and is the kind of 'witch'"—Bea used air quotes to emphasize her disgust with our cat-napping nemesis—"that gives the rest of us a bad name. How can you say 'poor girl'?"

Sitting down calmly, Aunt Astrid pushed her long locks behind her and looked sternly at her daughter. "Sit down, Bea."

Taking a seat next to me, Bea looked at her mother curiously.

"What you saw, Cath, are what we call witches' vials. This girl is not a witch, but she's obviously very scared of one."

Aunt Astrid went on to explain that during the days when people would see witches around every corner sabotaging crops, causing diseases, and stealing children and husbands, the fearful would use witches' vials. The person fearful of the witch would fill the jar with urine, nail clippings, hair, sometimes a scrap of clothing, sometimes drops of blood, small pieces of skin like a hangnail or a scab, then seal it tight. The jars were then set near all the entrances, preventing witches from crossing the thresholds.

"There are various ways witches' vials can affect a witch. If Bea were to go there and try and get close, she might get lost and turned around. If I went there, it might make me forget who I am and what I was doing there in the first place. In your instance, it made you nauseated."

"Seriously nauseated. I'm still feeling it." I rubbed my belly. "I also couldn't talk to Marshmallow or Treacle for that matter."

"I believe it. It's like mountains in the way of using a cell phone," Aunt Astrid explained. "The signals you are used to get cut off. Nothing can pass. This little girl just put a big mountain in our way. She must have a very scary reason for doing so."

"But what about the broom?" Bea asked. "Cath said she put a broom down in front of the door. What does that mean?"

"This girl is no dummy. She has obviously done her research." Aunt Astrid started to slice herself a piece of pie, and I had to look away. I couldn't handle the sight of food yet. "When people thought there was a witch in their village, some of them would put their broomsticks across their thresholds at night-time. Because witches were supposed to use these things to fly around on if they came across one lying on the floor, they were forced to count each bristle. By the time they actually counted them all, it was believed the sun would be on the rise, and the witch would be unable to complete her evil deeds."

"So, would that have happened to me? If I didn't get all shades of queasy, would I have been forced to count the bristles? That sounds crazy." I rubbed my head, feeling the sickness from my stomach traveling up the back of my neck. A headache was quickly approaching.

"I'm afraid so," Aunt Astrid said, taking a big bite of pie.

"And I'd have had no control? How can that be? I mean, what if this girl decides to render us power-less by throwing brooms at us, and we're compelled to count every bristle?" I was getting angry. First, the woman had my cat, which was bad enough. Then she put out witches' vials and thousand-bristled broom-sticks to compel us to count, and she is the poor girl? I was starting to wonder if someone had put a hex on Aunt Astrid.

"More importantly, how are we going to get to this girl?" Bea asked. "We obviously need to talk to her. A witch did that to Brit Clegg's father, but Brit isn't the witch. So who is?"

"Well, we can't get to her at her place. We might have to bring in the reserves." Aunt Astrid took another bite of pie. In four forkfuls, the dessert was almost gone. Where my aunt put it was anyone's guess because she still had quite a cute, soft figure for a woman her age.

We both looked at Bea, who rolled her eyes. "How am I going to nonchalantly tell Jake that Brit Clegg, the daughter of the man who died of one hell of a heart attack, has weird and quite offensive witches' vials all around her trailer home and also has Treacle?" She put her hands on her hips. "He'll hit the roof if he knows that we're sneaking up behind him on this case."

"I think we need to handle this the way we'd handle Darla Castellan." Aunt Astrid pushed herself up from her seat, reaching over to cut another piece of pie.

"You mean with a whip and a chair?" I asked as Aunt Astrid placed the plate in front of me. As soon as she did, my headache was gone, my neck relaxed, and my stomach grumbled with hunger. "How did you know?"

"It is also pretty common that the effects of witches' vials only last a couple of hours. Enough to keep us off our balance but not enough to keep us laid up for long. Besides, the color just came back into your cheeks." She gave me a wink that made me feel special.

I ate the pie and listened to Aunt Astrid's plan for getting Brit Clegg away from her home and some-place we could talk to her. "It's so simple, it has to work." I wiped my mouth after practically inhaling my dessert. I just needed a hamburger or something to wash it down.

"Bea, I think you should be the one to contact her. You have a natural way about you that sets people at ease," Aunt Astrid said.

I furrowed my brows after hearing this. "Wait a second. I can put people at ease. I am quite a people pleaser when it comes down to it."

Both women looked at me as if I were a baby babbling incoherent words into the middle of their adult discussion.

"No," was all Aunt Astrid said.

I shrugged, giving Bea a wink. The truth was I knew she was much more diplomatic and, well, just kinder than I ever was. I remembered my parents being good, loving people, but I didn't remember if either of them had a temper or what their limits were. I always had the feeling I developed my pattern of harsh, scratchy behavior after realizing how fate had cheated me.

808

After another slice of pie, some strong coffee, a bagel with cream cheese, and some leftover veggie chili, I was feeling much more like my regular self. Yet I couldn't shake the weird cottony feeling still in my head. It was as if a small corner existed in my mind in which the light couldn't penetrate. No matter how hard I reached and stretched inside my head, I couldn't get to that corner, but something was telling me I needed to see what was there.

I left Bea and Aunt Astrid alone to devise a plan in which Brit Clegg would bring me my cat. I couldn't help because my idea was to stomp over there, nauseated or not, and pound the door down. If she believed witches were so bad, I was more than happy to prove her right. She would be called some very nasty names and told to stay away from my cat and me. I'd also slam the door, if given the chance, and stomp away with a scowl on my face that she wouldn't soon forget. Yup! That would teach her.

Still, Treacle hadn't looked hurt or in pain. The worst thing for him was probably staying cooped up all day and night. If I knew my cat, he'd probably already introduced his claws to her upholstery and curtains. *Serves her right.* But if she didn't like witches, I hoped she wasn't going to take it out on Treacle. He couldn't help it that he was an exceptional black cat.

My eyes filled with tears. Treacle didn't see me last night, and I couldn't call to him. He hadn't even known I was there. What really bothered me was thinking that Treacle might think I wasn't looking for him. That thought broke my heart the most.

I made my way down Bryn Mawr Avenue and took a left onto First Street. There were dozens of little shops and restaurants to look into. The pedestrian traffic was bustling. I looked into the windows of the shops, thinking of nothing and everything at the same time. When I came to Standee's twenty-four-hour diner, I peeked in and saw two faces I knew.

I went inside and walked up to Jake and Blake, who sat at the counter sipping coffee. "Are you guys off duty? I promise I won't tell Bea and Aunt Astrid you're getting coffee and lunch at a place that's not the Brew-Ha-Ha."

"Hey, Cath. Want to join us? We're technically getting dinner then heading home. Had a wild morning." Jake was a handsome guy. Bea was very lucky because as pretty as he was on the outside, he was even more so on the inside. He was the big brother I never had.

"You know, I just ate at Aunt Astrid's." I patted my stomach. "So what kind of excitement did you guys have?"

"An 808 at the Walona Motel," Blake said after he took a sip of water. He was always so stiff.

"Okay, what is an 808, and what is the Walona Motel?"

"Disturbing the peace. The Walona Motel is over in the industrial part of town. It's on a side street just before you get on the expressway."

"The Walona Motel? I've never heard of it, but it sounds like a respite station for kings. What happened?"

"Apparently, two occupants of two separate rooms decided they didn't care to share the same air space with each other," Jake said as the waitress behind the counter served up big cheeseburgers in front of him and Blake. "A loud shouting match between a woman who was there by herself and another woman who was there with her husband. Nobody was drunk. No one had any priors. It just got loud. The woman and her husband said they'd be leaving, so there was no need for us to do anything."

"Well, that doesn't sound so bad," I said. "With the way the world is, it could have been a lot worse."

"Well, it was over and done with for me, but Blake here had a little more on his hands than just an ornery woman." Jake chuckled and nudged Blake with his elbow just before he took a big bite out of his burger.

"Really, was she looking for a stone ornament for her yard?" I asked, completely serious.

Blake looked at me then shook his head. "Some people in the world are just a little lonely. That's all."

"Or desperate," I mumbled. "Well, I gotta run. I'll tell Bea you're on your way home."

"Well, if you wait, I'll drop you wherever you're headed," Jake offered.

I shook my head. "No. I don't know if Bea told you, but Treacle hasn't come home for a few days." Technically, it was true, but I couldn't tell him any more than that, nor could I tell him anything about the mystery rolling around in my head like a silver pinball.

"That's the big black cat I see at the Brew-Ha-Ha, right?" Blake asked, looking at me oddly.

"Yeah, that's him. He's a prowler. He has all his claws, and he never likes being indoors for very long. But usually he's come back by now. I'm just strolling around, hoping maybe I'll see him." It wasn't a total lie but more like a lie of omission.

"Well, I usually take a ten-mile run at the end of the day to get centered," Blake said. "I'll keep an eye out on the south side of town for you." His eyes were serious, and there wasn't any of the cold hardness that was usually there.

"I'd appreciate that, Blake. Thank you."

"I lost a pet once. When I was a kid, we had an English bulldog named Buddy. We think someone stole him."

My heart just broke at the simple tragedy. He said it quickly, but I could tell it held a certain amount of weight in his heart. When I looked him in the eyes, he didn't look away. I saw the shadow of a memory there, then just as quickly, it was gone. He was back to Detective Blake Samberg and just the facts.

"How terrible." I put my hand over my heart.

For a moment, we looked at each other. He looked at me as if he were surprised I would say something so kind. I felt bad about that and wondered if he'd become a cop, and then detective, in order to help other people find their lost Buddies.

"Nothing worse." The right side of his mouth curled up in a sad grin.

"Right." I nodded. "Well, I better let you guys finish your lunches." I smiled at Jake and couldn't help feel my eyes drawn to Blake's. He was still looking at me a little more intently than usual. I don't know what was going on behind his eyes, but they were deeper than I had noticed before.

Brit

A couple of days had passed since Aunt Astrid and Bea put their plan into motion. It was a very simple idea, but we'd have no way of knowing if it worked until Brit Clegg showed up at the café.

"Did you offer her a free lunch, too?" I'd asked when they first told me they had sent her a letter.

"No," Bea said. "We told her the truth."

"What?" I hissed over the counter at the Brew-Ha-Ha.

As I looked to see if anyone had noticed my outburst, Bea took my hand. "I told her we were sorry what happened to her father. We were sorry she was afraid, but that we knew what she was afraid of and wanted to help."

"What about Treacle?"

"Of course. We told her we knew she had a cat that didn't belong to her, and unless she wanted the authorities involved, she'd bring the cat with her."

"And when is she supposed to arrive here?"

"Today. We told her we're open from seven in the morning until eight o'clock at night. We said we understand people have to work and that she probably had many details to tend to. We said we didn't want to inconvenience her, yet at the same time, we had to talk to her."

I took a deep breath. "Well, that sounds like you were real nice. I think she might come."

Bea shrugged and widened her eyes. It was a crap shoot, but what other choice did we have?

All day long, every time the bells over the door jingled their happy little tune, Aunt Astrid, Bea and I looked up to see if it was a woman carrying a cat box. Every time, we were disappointed.

It wasn't until we were serving our last evening customers at ten minutes before eight that the door opened and the frantic "meow, meow, meow" that had been so familiar to me snapped my head toward the door.

"Treacle!" I cried out loud. *"Treacle, are you all*

right?" I called to him inside my head. *"Are you hurt at all? I missed you so much!"*

"Cath!" he meowed loudly. *"You won't believe what is happening! I was afraid I might never see you again!"*

"Hi. Hi. You must be Brit," I said quickly. As much as I wanted to be mad at this girl, looking in her eyes, I couldn't help but feel sorry for her. Her expression was a mixture of sadness, fear, and strength. No matter what had happened with her father, something else was going on that had her on edge and ready to fight.

She nodded and handed me the cardboard cat carrier. From the little air holes, a black paw kept sticking out, reaching and scratching for me. All anyone else could hear were wild and continual meows. I heard the relief and happiness coming from my beloved companion.

"Please, sit down," I said, looking at Bea and Aunt Astrid, who were coming around the counter.

"I can't stay," she said curtly. Her eyes bounced from Bea to Astrid to me and back again. She wasn't just nervous. She was also very, very scared.

"Brit Clegg? It's really nice to meet you. Thank you so much for coming," Bea said with her hand stretched out for Brit to shake.

The girl looked at Bea's dainty, pretty hand as if it were a claw and nervously took half a step backward.

"Honey, believe me when I tell you you are safe here," Bea said gently.

"Very safe, dear." Aunt Astrid stepped up with her hands folded neatly in front of her. "Your father was our friend. We did business with him. It was a sad day when we heard he had passed."

I studied Brit's face and could tell she was doing something I was familiar with. She was biting her tongue so she wouldn't cry. How many times had I done that when I was young, and a memory of my mother came vividly into view? When a smell or sound came out of nowhere and sent me whirling back to when I was a kid, I would ache inside even as an adult. Then I'd bite my tongue so I wouldn't cry.

The furry paw of my friend pushed through a space at the top of the box to touch my hand, and I took him to a table away from the ladies. I barely had the top open before Treacle leapt into my arms, rubbing his soft head under my chin and along my face as his claws poked into my shirt and pricked my skin. He acted as though he couldn't get close enough to me, and I hugged him back, kissing the top of his head, rocking him gently, and listening to his happy motor purring the whole while.

"I was so worried," I said in my mind, feeling tears in my eyes.

"I was so scared she was going to take me away. I couldn't talk to her. I didn't know why she had me. Then I thought I saw you, but I couldn't hear you. I was afraid."

Squeezing tighter, I held the big black ball of fur in my arms and stroked his head. *"You're going to have to lie low for a while, Treacle. Until we figure out what is going on, you're staying in the house. There are two other scaredy cats who've been worried to death over you."*

"I miss my friends."

"Well, be sure to thank Marshmallow. She was the one who found the trailer."

"How?" Treacle asked. *"How could she see it?"*

"She came with me on a whim. She could see an aura around the place that I would have never seen. You didn't see her when you peeked out the window?"

"I thought maybe the female was bringing you to me."

"Was she mean to you?"

"No. She was kind. But she is afraid of something, and that made me more afraid. And I think we should all be afraid."

I swallowed hard and looked at Brit Clegg as Aunt Astrid and Bea tried to talk to her.

Then Brit started to get loud. "I'm not staying," she said sternly. "I have to go."

"We just want to talk to you," Bea said, and I could tell she hoped to touch Brit's sleeve or hand. "You aren't in any trouble."

"Please," I said. "Let us put on some tea and fix you something to eat. We've got apple pie and some vegetarian chili and—"

"No." She looked at me sternly. "Don't let that cat out. Next time, it might not be me that gets a hold of him. Why you'd let a black cat roam around, I don't know. People don't like black cats."

I lowered Treacle back into the box. He lay down immediately, and I could tell he was exhausted.

"What do you mean?" I tried not to come across as scary or intimidating. "Treacle is a roamer. He's just a tomcat. He's been roaming the neighborhood since he was a kitten, and nothing—"

"If you love that cat"—her eyes filled with tears —"then you'll listen to me and keep him inside. Not everyone sees him the way you do." Brit grabbed the door and yanked.

"Wait!" Bea called after her. "Don't go. Please, we can help you. We know you're afraid of witches. We know there's one in Wonder Falls, and she's responsible for..." Bea couldn't bring herself to say the words. "We know she, or *he*, is responsible for what happened to your father."

Brit froze. Her body began to tremble. She looked over her shoulder at us. Tears soaked her cheeks. *"She,"* she hissed. Brit's eyes displayed the hatred she was feeling, and she clenched her teeth. "It's a she." She threw the door open and stomped out.

For a few seconds, none of us moved.

"Meow?" was the only noise that cut through the silence. I looked into the box and saw Treacle looking contentedly at me as I scratched his head. His green eyes blinked lazily, and his tail waved almost in slow motion.

"Well, that could have gone better," I said.

Witches Can Die Too

❦

Two days had passed since Brit had returned Treacle.

The black cat seemed to be happy inside for the first time since he was a kitten. As soon as he settled in, and I knew he was home and safe, I asked Treacle what had happened.

He climbed onto my lap and stretched his arms to either side of my neck as I stroked his short black fur. He looked at me intently. *"I was across town. Something was buzzing around there,"* he told me in his mind.

"What do you mean?"

Treacle licked his nose. *"My usual felines would tell me what was going on, but I couldn't find anyone. They were all hiding. They wouldn't come out, but they peeked out from corners and shadows."*

"You didn't think maybe you should get out of there?"

"I saw the gray cat with the scar. I don't like him. We usually fight. He seemed to know something, but he wouldn't tell me. He growled low at me as I approached him. Not his usual fighting growl but more like he was mad I was giving away his hiding place." Treacle's claws poked from soft paws as he continued his tale. *"I should have run. I should have hid like the other cats, but I didn't."*

"Oh, my poor boy," I soothed, rubbing his head behind his ears and stroking his back.

He continued his story. *"The next thing I knew, I couldn't see. Someone had covered me completely. I scratched and bit and tried to move. I screamed. I cried. But I was pulled off the ground. I was in something... a sack. I didn't have a lot of room, and I couldn't see anything. Nothing I did seemed to help. I was being carried away."*

The thought of Treacle being taken away against his will, violently, cruelly, and brought to a strange place, tore at my heart. My eyes filled with tears.

"When I was finally free of the confines, I was in a place like this," Treacle said, looking around our home.

"You were in her trailer."

"Her trailer, yes. She'd never had a cat there. She fed me and tried to pet me." Treacle scooted closer to me, so close his whiskers rubbed against my cheek as he nuzzled his head along my jaw. *"But she wasn't you."*

I scratched the back of his head and neck.

"I missed you, Cath."

"You have no idea how much I missed you, big kitty." I hugged him, letting my tears fall into his shiny black fur and disappear. *"You're home now and safe. And tomorrow, we'll go visit your friends Marshmallow and Peanut Butter. They've been so worried about you."*

"I've missed them," he purred.

Treacle fell asleep next to me on the couch. I stretched out, putting my feet up and stuffing my favorite throw pillow behind my head. Every time I moved even slightly, it set off Treacle's purring mechanism, and he'd start buzzing happily, his eyes still closed.

I must have been more tired than I thought because I fell asleep within just a few minutes. I was so grateful Treacle was safe and sound. Brit may have been weird and scared, but she didn't hurt him. What had she wanted with him? She'd gone through a lot of trouble if all she wanted was a cat.

And I couldn't help but wonder what she meant when she said not to let that cat out because next time it might not be her who got a hold of him.

That thought rolled around in my head as I fell asleep, leading me to a terrible dream. Treacle was gone again because I'd simply left the door open, something I'd never do in the waking world. I intentionally left my home vulnerable and Aunt Astrid's, too. Marshmallow was also gone because I'd left a door open.

In the dream, I didn't tell anyone it was my own negligence that led to the animals' disappearance. I held the guilt inside and pretended nothing was wrong until something made its way into my home.

The strange creature in the dream was human-like. It had two arms, two legs, and a head, but it was shrouded in a black robe that was dirty and worn and appeared to have been buried or left in the elements for several seasons.

I couldn't be sure, but I think there were living things on it… small, ugly, writhing living things that fell onto my beige carpet along with bits of dirt and twigs. Bony, white hands were all I could see.

On the right hand was a gaudy, obscene ring with a black gemstone and a rhinestone pentagram. Had the horrific creature decided it needed a little bling to be truly terrifying so it bedazzled a cheap, imitation gemstone ring?

I stared at the ring on the monster's hand as it proceeded to crawl through my open bedroom window. It was pulling itself through in a grotesque manner that made me think of someone having a convulsion. I didn't try to stop it. I was paralyzed and could only watch as it pulled itself farther and farther into my home. Finally, it stopped its horrible jerking movements and looked at me.

Underneath its shroud was a ghostly pale face with empty, black sockets where the eyes should be. As I stared at its face, the thing laughed. It sounded like the voice of a classroom bully, a heartless child mocking another. And the voice was even more terrifying than the face because it was unnatural.

The whole thing was unnatural.

When I opened my mouth to scream, all I could hear was the hiss of a cat.

My eyes snapped open, and I felt my heart pounding. My skin was wet, and as I blinked, my familiar room came into focus. But the hissing sent my body into a spasm that jerked me clear off the couch and to my feet.

It was Treacle. He was in my bedroom. He stood stone still on the floor about two feet away from the bedroom window. Then I heard it. Scratching. In my head, I tried to remember if I had left the window open or closed the night before. I was pretty sure it was closed as I listened again.

I tiptoed to the bedroom door entrance and placed my hands on either side of the frame to steady myself. Luckily, the window was closed.

Treacle slowly arched his back. Every single strand of his jet black fur stood on edge, making him look as though he were at least ten pounds more cat than he actually was. Whatever was making those scratching noises was not supposed to be there.

The scratching was slow and long as if whoever or whatever was doing it was scraping its claw, fingers, talons, or something from the top of the window diagonally across to the opposite bottom corner.

Treacle's whiskers twitched, his eyes unblinking as a serious, mean growl came from deep inside his gut. The creature at the window was more than just a squirrel or chipmunk getting too close to Treacle's personal space. Whatever was outside was something dangerous.

"What is it, Trea?" I asked, carefully whispering with my thoughts.

"I don't know," he said, still growling. *"But it's out there, and it wants to be in here."*

We both stood perfectly still. I don't know about Treacle, but I held my breath, focusing intently on whether I could hear any other noise besides the scratching. I remembered the image from my nightmare that had snapped me awake, and I began to sweat.

It couldn't have been a premonition. I didn't have that gift. Aunt Astrid was the one who could see future possibilities, not me. My dream was probably just a collection of all the things that had been going on, right? There wasn't going to be some disgusting, eyeless form with maggots and worms on its clothes pushing through my bedroom window, right? And if there were, Aunt Astrid would have seen it already, right?

Well, she would if she were looking, but if she were distracted and looking in another direction, then who knows?

I let out my breath and felt winded. Just as I was about to take a step inside the room, Treacle bolted to the window. He was up and underneath the curtain within a split second, hissing, clawing, and scratching at the glass. Not wanting my precious pet to get hurt, I forced myself to move.

Throwing back the curtain, I watched as Treacle continued to scratch at the glass, growling and hissing. Then I looked up to where his eyes were focused and saw nothing.

Growing up in a witch's family instilled a few

rules in my head that most kids probably wouldn't think twice about. One rule was that seeing wasn't always believing. Sometimes, we believed in things greater than ourselves, even though we may not have been able to see those things.

But as puny humans, we were terrified of things we couldn't see. All I could see was the little patch of green grass outside my bedroom window along with the nearby tree line.

I squinted into the foliage and saw nothing... no cluster of moving shadows outlining a human form, no eyes peering back at me, nothing. But Treacle was still going mad.

Leaning closer to the window, I pulled the curtains back to see if I was missing something.

BANG! BANG! BANG! BANG! Someone was pounding on my front door. The blows were so loud and hard that Treacle and I jumped a good foot into the air.

"Why is someone knocking like that? I have a doorbell," I said more to calm myself than to actually get an answer.

I looked at Treacle, who seemed to have calmed a little. He sniffed around the edges of the window, his eyes scanning the yard. Whatever had been out there was either gone or suddenly not so menacing. Treacle perched himself on the small ledge and stood as my sturdy and true lookout.

Tiptoeing to the front door, I had already made the decision not to answer it. No way was I just going to pull the door open. I squatted down to see if I could make out the shadow of feet across the bottom threshold, then I stood and stretched my neck to see if a shadow could be seen pulling away from the peephole.

I saw nothing. I turned my head and listened. Then I heard a swish sound coming from beneath the door.

Treacle was at my side in an instant, hissing madly. Both of us stood there, stepping closer to see what was inching its way underneath the door.

"Should I rush the door and yank it open?" I asked out loud.

"No," Treacle said then made a dash for the bedroom again.

I swallowed hard and watched. It was paper. Just paper. A note was worming its way through the narrow slash of space between the door and my foyer floor. I'd never been so terrified as I was watching the scene unfold in front of me. It felt as if I were watching a film being run in reverse, in which rain fell upward, and people backed out of doors. Our brains were conditioned to recognize when something felt wrong.

I listened for Treacle and heard the *thump-thump* of his tail whipping on the floor as he sat studying something. I looked at the front door, half expecting it to explode inward or pulse as though it were alive. But it didn't. It remained a normal door.

"Stop being silly," I said to myself. "Whoever is dropping off notes is obviously more scared of you than you are of them."

That line of complete bologna made me feel a lot better. Sometimes, I impressed myself with my own words and how I could encourage myself. I walked up to the door, bent down, swiped up the note, and took several careful steps back, just in case.

My hands trembled. What I saw was shocking and obscene. Letters cut out of magazines formed a jagged message that looked as dangerous as the threat:

Stay away from Brit.
Witches can die, too.

The message was bad enough, but the handwritten scribbles at the bottom froze me to my core. Next to a cutout magazine picture of a black cat on a silver platter with its head separated from the body, someone had scrawled,

The cat will be mine.

Boiling Blood

❧

Terror and anger filled me. I wasn't sure what emotion won out. I was terrified that someone knew we were looking into Marvin Clegg's death, and that the person was most likely the killer and a witch. The fact that the hag would threaten my cat made my blood boil.

Treacle snapped me out of my conflict. He was in the bedroom again, growling and scratching the glass.

"What? What is it?" I called to him.

"Outside! It's out there!"

Darting into the bedroom, I threw aside the curtains with more anger than I expected then stopped. It was a cat. I had never seen him around before. He was just sitting there, staring at us.

Normally, a cat would blink, a muscle would twitch, or its nostrils would flare as it picked up a scent. But I wasn't looking at a normal cat. The black-and-white tuxedo cat with intense green eyes *looked* like an average cat, but there was a hollowness in its eyes. Something else was there... something sinister.

I heard Treacle calling to it. He said he'd seen it before around the trailer park. The tuxedo cat would slink underneath trailers, around cars and garbage cans, and climb on top of mailboxes and makeshift fences so it could stare at Treacle when he was at Brit's. The cat never spoke to him, and it wasn't speaking to me either. It just sat there as if it were studying us.

"Treacle?"

"Yes?"

"Why did you say it's *out there?"*

"Because that's what it is. It's not a feline. It's an it.*"*

My body shook. I had the sneaking suspicion this creature could hear our thoughts and just chose not to speak.

I don't know how long Treacle and I stood there trying to stare down the creature in front of us, but the tuxedo cat seemed to become more and more menacing with each passing second.

The *ping, ping, ping* of my phone made the two of us jump. I ran into the front room, grabbed the phone quickly, and ran back to the bedroom to look out the window. It was gone.

"Where is it?" I asked Treacle, who had stayed in the bedroom.

"I don't know. I looked at you leaving the room, and when I looked back, it was gone."

I pulled the cord on the slatted blinds, letting them fall all the way to the floor then made sure the curtains were in place before answering the phone.

Bea was beside herself on the end of the line. "She threatened Jake!"

"What? Who did?" I suddenly forgot about our furry, glass-eyed visitor and sat on the edge of my bed.

"The witch. She threatened Jake. Said what happened to Marvin could easily happen to him if we didn't back off and leave Brit alone. She left a note under our front door."

My heart flipped over in my chest. "When did you get this note?" I already knew the answer.

"Just... now. Just a few seconds ago. Jake went running outside to see if he could catch the person, but there wasn't a soul in sight."

"Was there a cat around?"

Bea sniffled on the other end then I heard her stop as though she were thinking. "A cat? I don't know. Why?"

"I got a note, too. Just now. At this very moment. It said she was going to get Treacle."

Bea gasped on the other end and shouted to Jake, repeating what I had just told her. "Jake said you and Treacle need to get over here quick. He's going to go get my mom in the squad car."

"Make sure she brings Marshmallow. I don't think any of our companions are safe from this witch."

Just then, Treacle made such a loud crying noise that Bea was able to hear it on the other end. "Cath, what's going on over there?" Bea cried into the phone.

"Oh no." I pressed the phone hard to my ear as the shade snapped all the way up to the ceiling, and the curtain fell to the floor. The black-and-white cat sat right in front of the glass staring inside at Treacle.

"What it sees, she knows!" Treacle hissed then snapped. He would have flown through the window and fought with everything he had if he were able. But I wasn't going to give him the job of defending the house. That was my job.

I turned and stomped to the foyer with the phone still in my hand, grabbed an umbrella from the stand, and was about to yank open the door when I froze. "Bea?"

"Cath, what is it? Oh, talk to me. All I can hear is Treacle hissing and meowing."

"I was about to open the door and chase this other cat away when something in me told me not to. It wants us separated. It wants my cat. Whatever this thing is wants my cat, and I don't think it will let anything stand in its way."

"Then you guys pack a bag and get over here."

"Yes. Yes. We're on our way, Bea. We're leaving right now."

"Okay. We'll see you in a few minutes. If it takes any longer, I'm sending all of Wonder Falls P.D. to get you."

"We're already out the door." I scooped up my keys and Treacle before I even hung up the phone.

Threats

✻

I carried Treacle in my arms rather than a carrier. Just in case we met with any kind of trouble, I wanted him to be able to get away, to defend himself... just in case I wasn't able to. The thought sent a shiver down my back.

"*I wouldn't leave you,*" he said. "*Not if you needed me.*"

"*I wouldn't leave you either, pretty kitty.*" I let out a deep breath. The closer I walked to Bea and Jake's place, the better I started to feel. I reached the front of their house just as Jake pulled in behind me. Aunt Astrid was in the front seat next to him holding Marshmallow.

Thank goodness she brought her cat, too. The whole family was underneath one roof, and I knew what kind of power we had together. I hoped the evil witch, wherever she was, got a good, long look at us. We weren't just a couple of teenagers dabbling in mischief.

"Hey, Cath," Jake said, getting out of the car.

I waved and walked over to help Aunt Astrid. Bea stood in the doorway, holding the door open for everyone. We set our cats down, and they quickly pranced into the door, where Peanut Butter was eagerly waiting for them.

Once we were all inside, Jake locked the door. He kissed Bea on the cheek and went upstairs.

"Where's he going?" I asked quietly.

"He's going to take a shower then go to work," Bea said. "Blake is stopping by to pick him up."

Bea looked at me oddly when she mentioned that Blake was coming by to pick up Jake, but she quickly busied herself with pouring water into a copper kettle.

I hadn't seen Blake since he spoke to me about losing his own pet. I looked at my reflection in the glass on the microwave door and smoothed my hair little.

"I think we have a real issue here, ladies." Aunt Astrid sat on a stool next to the long counter.

"Did you get a note, too?" I asked.

She nodded.

"What did it say?"

Aunt Astrid waved her hand. "Oh, not much different from you both. A lot of huff and puff. The problem is this witch thinks she knows what she's doing. She's careless and sloppy and yet has found a connection to the darkest elements that are working for her." Aunt Astrid pinched her lips together.

I helped myself to a bottle of water from Bea's fridge and took a seat next to Aunt Astrid. "Have you told Jake any of this?" I asked carefully.

Bea and Jake had just recovered from some bumpy growing pains, and they both vowed not to keep secrets from each other anymore. Jake knew Bea was a witch, he knew she had a rare and beautiful gift of healing, and he knew witchcraft ran in her family. But I wasn't sure he was ready to know we suspected the death of Marvin Clegg to be murder, not just a heart attack.

"Yes. I told him about Levi, the morgue, and Brit and Treacle. He grumbled at first." Bea placed the kettle on the stove. "But he said as long as none of us were breaking the law, he wasn't worried. However, this note changes things." She folded her arms across her chest.

"Brit Clegg knows who this is, but she isn't going

to tell us." I took a long drink from my water bottle. "At least not without some serious coaxing, and even then, I don't think she'd crack."

I looked over to the sitting area of the kitchen and saw Peanut Butter, Marshmallow, and Treacle lying close to each other, their eyes narrow slits, their breathing slow and calm, and their tails waving lazily. Peanut Butter kept touching Treacle with his paw every couple of minutes, wanting to make sure Treacle was still there. I could hear them talking. They were discussing the tuxedo cat that had been staring at Treacle through the window. Just the thought of that *thing* sent a shiver up my spine.

"Did Jake offer any advice?" Aunt Astrid asked. "A fresh set of eyes on this might be just what we need."

"Actually, his advice was that if Levi started all this, maybe he should be the one to handle it."

"I'm all for passing this off onto some unsuspecting schlub to deal with. Exploding hearts, death threats, cat-napping... count me out." I stood and went to look in Bea's cupboards for a snack.

"That isn't a bad idea," Aunt Astrid said, standing and grabbing her big purse from the floor where she'd dropped it.

The lovely, vintage carpetbag purse was similar to

the one Mary Poppins had carried. And just like Mary Poppins, Aunt Astrid could pull dozens and dozens of oddly shaped items of all sizes out of her purse. Right then, she pulled out her all-purpose spell book. Doctors referred to the Merck Manual to look up lists of symptoms that helped them narrow down the cause of an ailment. Aunt Astrid could sort of do the same with her lofty tome.

"You're kidding, right?" I asked. "You're not going to hand this over to Levi. He doesn't even know he's a medium, let alone know how to do battle with a black witch who got her witchcraft degree off the back of a matchbook."

I shoveled some salt-free, gluten-free pretzels into my mouth then grimaced and spat them into the garbage. "Don't you have any real food?"

"There's one thing you're all missing," said Jake's deep voice from the hallway.

He was standing there dressed in a nice pair of dark gray slacks and a white button-down shirt. He walked behind Bea, gave her a playful pinch on the butt as he passed, then opened the cupboard, reaching up where I couldn't see. "This person sent you all threats. She had to take the time to cut out the letters and glue them down."

He pulled out a bag of Doritos, full of salt and fat

and all the things I loved, and handed them to me with a wink.

"So that proves she knows where we all live." Bea shook her head at Jake's stash.

"Right," Jake agreed. "So if she was so good at what she supposedly can do, making hearts explode and whatnot, why couldn't she have done it to you guys? It would have looked like nothing more than a freakish coincidence."

The doorbell chimed a happy little ding-dong, and Jake went to answer it.

"Check the peephole!" Bea yelled to him before he opened the door. He did just that then yelled back to us that it was all clear. After he opened the door, I heard him say hello to Blake.

When Blake came into the kitchen, he nodded at Aunt Astrid and Bea. Once again, I got the royal treatment… a judgmental once-over. I blinked in an attempt to hide how I rolled my eyes in annoyance then shoved a couple of Doritos into my mouth.

"Hello, Detective," Aunt Astrid said, closing her book and reaching her hand out to shake. "It's nice to see you again."

"You as well, Mrs. Greenstone. Looks like you're doing some heavy reading there." He nodded at her spell book but didn't look very closely at it.

"Just a book of family recipes. Trying to help Cath learn how to cook." She smiled happily at the detective. I was shocked when I saw the right side of his mouth curl up a little.

"Well, good luck." He was probably completely unaware that his reply was totally obnoxious. Not that it mattered. His response made Bea and Aunt Astrid laugh.

"I know how to cook," I mumbled. Turning around, I tossed the Doritos bag back up on the shelf for Jake.

"You boys be careful out there tonight. Extra careful," Bea said, pulling on Jake's strong arm until he bent down far enough for her to kiss his cheek.

"Don't worry. We'll be fine." Both men left, talking about some sporting event or news story they'd heard as if tonight were no different from any other night.

Bea let out a big sigh and drummed her fingers on the counter. Finally, she turned on the stove, and within minutes, the teapot was whistling happily.

She had already prepared two cups, knowing I didn't drink tea, and poured the hot liquid over the little mesh bags. I hated to admit it, but it smelled wonderful... mint and lemon and something else I couldn't place. But I knew if I tasted the tea, it would be the same old hot water taste I always disliked.

"I don't understand how that man can be so calm when his life has been threatened. I'm a nervous wreck," Bea said.

Aunt Astrid patted her hand. "I cast a quick spell of protection over him in the car on the way over. He just thought I had a sneezing fit. It should get him through tonight's work all right. I am still not convinced this person we're dealing with really knows what she's doing."

"So, what should we do?" I asked.

"Well, Jake is right." Aunt Astrid casually leafed through her book of spells. "If this woman knew her stuff, why didn't she just use her magic? Instead, she resorted to scare tactics and threatening letters. It doesn't quite make sense."

"So what are you looking for?" I asked, peeking over my aunt's shoulder as she flipped through her book.

"I don't know yet, but I think a little extra protection for us and our feline friends is definitely in order."

Aunt Astrid hopped off her stool, reached into her bag, and pulled out some sage, a book of matches, and a black lace fan. Conducting a smudging ritual was easy and very effective in keeping away the spiritual creepy crawlies. Similar to how hedge apples kept spiders away, smudging filled a place with positive barriers. The ritual ensured all the juicy goodness stayed inside, while the evil parasites were left to starve from lack of energy on the outside.

Aunt Astrid lit the sage, a candle for Bea, and one for me. We followed her through the house as she fanned the pleasant-smelling herb into every room, into every corner of the floors and ceilings, around every window and door, until finally, the whole house felt light and airy.

The cats continued their vigil of lying and stretching across the carpet, bounding from chair to chair, and taking short naps. Every once in a while, I would catch Treacle looking out the sliding glass door into the yard. His fur never rose, but I could tell staying cooped up inside was starting to get to him.

He was a roamer, an alley cat deep down, and he longed for the freedom that came with chasing down mice, climbing fences, investigating strange parts of town, and talking with other felines. Even the occasional fight was in his blood. Watching him look outside, hearing him take a deep breath then letting it out listlessly, broke my heart.

It was one thing for someone to go after people. We've been screwing up our own lives since man first began to walk upright and utter the word "no." But to go after an animal that only longed to do what it was created to do? A person who would do that was a certain kind of evil for which there were no words.

Levi

W e had to find out who was behind all this. And as if those words had made a complete circle through the cosmos, we were all pleasantly surprised the next day to see Levi Cummings walk through the door of the café.

Aunt Astrid and I had spent the night at Bea's house. Jake preferred being at the station at night until early morning and apparently, so did Blake.

Bea had tried to tell me that Blake Samberg was really a very pleasant fellow. He was alone, no family to speak of, very intelligent, and not one to throw around his emotions as if he might need them for an emergency later. He liked to read and think about things very intently.

Bea and Jake had had him over for dinner a couple of times. It was a custom among those who worked in the police department to do that sort of thing to get to know one another. They were, in a way, responsible for each other, so spending time together helped develop that weird bond so many cops had. The bond often didn't just save their lives but their sanity as well.

Like a caravan of gypsies, Aunt Astrid, Bea, and I traveled to the café, leaving the cats at home all together. There was strength in numbers for us as well as for them. We had stayed up late talking and going over everything we knew to see if there was anything we'd missed.

Aunt Astrid tried to use the threats we'd each received to locate the person who sent them, to get a name, a face, or anything that might be helpful. But the psychic energy around the messages was so messy and disorganized, it was like trying to read poetry written by a five-year-old.

I talked with Treacle to see if he remembered anything from being at Brit's house that might help us. But there was nothing.

We felt like we'd hit a dead end, that is, until we saw Levi saunter in. Aunt Astrid was at his side almost immediately.

"Well, hello, Levi. How are you feeling?" she asked in her most innocent and disarming matronly voice.

"Hi, Mrs. Greenstone. I'm doing just fine." He smiled down at her.

"We were a little worried about you the last time you paid us a visit."

He shook his head, and seemed a little embarrassed. "It must have been something I ate. Not here, of course." He quickly tried to cover up his misstatement. "I mean, whatever it was just sort of snuck up on me. But I'll tell you what... after I got home, my head was clearer than it's ever been. Not sure if the two are related or not, but I'm feeling good."

"Well, that is good to hear. What can we get you?" Aunt Astrid asked.

"You know, I don't know what it is, but I have been trying to get here for the past couple of days, and my schedules and traffic and construction have all seemed to have been pointing me in another direction. I have had such a craving for your tea with the lavender-infused honey that I just said if I do nothing else today, I'm getting that tea."

Aunt Astrid hid the worry on her face. "Absolutely. Cath, would you get Levi a tea with honey while I sit and have a chat with him?"

"One specialty tea with special honey coming right up," I said, also aware of the game being played on Levi.

"The forces are working against him," Bea said. "He's been trying to get here, but something always prevented it. Here, give me that tea bag."

I handed Bea the little mesh baggie that smelled like apples, oranges, spice, mint, and some other soothing scents I didn't recognize. Bea pulled it open, and with a few waves of her hand, added some special guidance to the herbs so Levi would find his way safely to his next destination.

Aunt Astrid led Levi to the back table where she had first tried to perform her psychic reading on him. They sat back there for a little while. Bea and I didn't hear any shouting or arguing or anything. We assumed that was good.

About ten minutes passed. Levi's tea was steaming hot and ready. Finally, he came strolling up to the counter, looking as fit as a fiddle and quite in control of his faculties. He gave us both a cheery good-bye as he scooped up his tea and left the café.

"That was weird," I said. "Last time, he was

nearly carried out on a stretcher. This time, he skips out of here like a guy who just won the lottery."

Bea swallowed hard and went back to check on her mother. Aunt Astrid had not followed Levi to the front of the store. I waited on a few customers. The rush hour was coming to an end, and still neither Bea nor Aunt Astrid had come to the front. Finally, there was a break in the customers, and I scooted back to the round table in the cubby to see my aunt pale and shaking.

"There's going to be another murder," Aunt Astrid said.

Spiritual Informant

❧❧❧

Before Aunt Astrid could say anything else, we were called back to actually *work* at the café. A study group of about sixteen young people came in all at once. They each wanted something different, and they took up just about every seat in the café. Once they left, the lunchtime rush came in.

As soon as things started to slow down, Min and Amalia paid us a visit, which was a refreshing and much-needed break from all the talk of mediums and murder. After they left, our after-work and evening crowd came in a steady stream until finally we turned around the CLOSED sign and locked the door.

Before I could speak, I saw a strange movement

outside the big window. I stepped a little closer and peered through the glass. I had to cup my hands around my eyes to cut down on the glare, then I saw a cat crossing the street. It froze for a second and looked my way. Then it darted into the shadows.

"What it sees, she knows!" I heard Treacle's warning in my head. I couldn't be sure it was the same tuxedo cat that had been at my house, but none of us were willing to take any chances. We all retreated to the safety of Bea's house.

"So, did Levi say who will get murdered?" I rocked slowly in the big swing on Bea's front porch. "Maybe give us directions to their house? Maybe tell us the name of the killer, too?"

Aunt Astrid sat in the wide-backed, wicker chair, staring into space but seeing something neither Bea nor I could. Bea stood across from me, leaning on the white banister that outlined her entire porch.

Aunt Astrid was obviously amazed by Levi's channeling ability, but she couldn't tell him about his particular gift. She didn't feel as if it were her place, plus it would open up the possibility that he could discover the true heritage of the Greenstone women. My aunt was not willing to risk our secret.

"It was as if someone had flipped a switch," she said, shaking her head in amazement. "He was completely unaware of the transition. It was seamless. One minute, he was smiling, plain old Levi Cummings, and the next..." She swallowed hard. "It just began. Whatever was communicating through him was just waiting, as though it knew it was in the spotlight."

She then described an experience I didn't think I'd ever want to encounter. I certainly didn't want to sit across the table, face-to-face, with whatever had become our informant.

Levi had taken his seat, and the second Aunt Astrid reached out to pat his hand, he gasped. He sucked in a great gulp of air as if he were afraid he might not get another one, and his eyes rolled over white. The corners of his mouth contorted into a vicious grimace, and he leaned in close to Aunt Astrid.

He was so close, she could not only feel his hot breath in her face, but she could hear the echoes from the dimension in which the entity was poking through. She heard other sounds, too... clicks, buzzes, and whispers from unseen spirits that may have hoped to tell their own tales.

"It's going to happen again," Levi said—well, not Levi, but our spirit informant. "All those cars driving by, and no one sees. It will happen again."

"What will happen again?" Aunt Astrid asked.

Levi's body began to jerk back and forth just enough to be unsettling. Something laughed through Levi, but the laugh sounded more like a hiss.

"Death. It surrounds her. She summons it, and it will burst through like it did before. And she wants that cat!"

"Wait!" I said, interrupting the story. "He said that? He said this person wants Treacle? What for?" My eyes brimmed with tears. I had never worried about Treacle before. Letting him out to roam was part of our routine. It was innocent, and we trusted each other, but someone was trying to ruin that. Treacle would go crazy if I kept him inside all the time. How dare someone do that to us? How dare she.

When Aunt Astrid nodded, Bea quickly came to my side and slipped her arm around my shoulder. We listened to the rest of my aunt's story.

"I asked it *who*. I asked it to tell me who was going to die. Who was going to be put through this agony?" She brushed her hair from her face and looked out onto the darkening street, which was quiet and peaceful. "All it would say was that the daughter knows. And that she was going to suffer for it."

"She'll do it again," Levi had jeered. "She'll keep doing it. She doesn't know how to stop, and she won't even try."

"And that was the end of it. Levi's face became his soft, unassuming self, and his eyes were back seeing this world and not clouded by the other's visions. The poor boy asked me what I'd been talking about as his mind seemed to have just drifted off on its own for a second."

"So, when are we going to Brit's place?" Bea asked, standing from the swing and brushing off her pants.

"Yeah, I'm ready now if you ladies are." I pushed myself off the seat with a grunt. Bea always was the more ladylike of the two of us.

"I agree, Cath." Aunt Astrid smoothed out her gypsy-style skirt. She looked like a fortuneteller, exotic and mysterious. You'd never guess she could fling you across the room with the wave of her hand and a few chosen words if she absolutely had to.

"Mom, maybe you should sit this one out. It's going to be a mess, I can just tell. From what Cath described and what I have seen so far, I have the feeling the psychic backwash is going to be darn near revolting. And—"

"I was thinking the same thing, Bea, honey, but about you."

"Me? What for? I can help."

"Of course you can, my dear. But the facts are that Cath knows how to get there, and I'm the only one here with the strength to combat those witches' vials. If she made them correctly, and from the sound of it, she has, then neither one of you would be strong enough to get past them. Plus,"—she stepped up to her daughter and cupped Bea's chin in her hand—"if anything happens to Jake, you have to be here, and the cats must also remain here."

"Won't you please take care of Treacle? Make sure he doesn't get out or that anyone gets a hold of him?" My gut felt tight when I asked Bea to do that for me. On one hand, I worried about Treacle. On the other hand, I worried about myself. Those witches' vials knocked me out, and I was not looking forward to encountering them again.

Skala

With much trepidation, Aunt Astrid and I made our way to the trailer park, but this time, we drove through the main entrance.

We weren't there to skulk around in the shadows or sneak up on Brit. We were there to find out what we were dealing with. There was no time to play games.

The trailer park was dark, and crickets kept up their vigil in the nearby woods. Moths and June bugs circled lazily around the fluorescent lights, which gave off a queasy green light matching my complexion at the moment.

"I can feel it already." Aunt Astrid pointed in the

direction I needed to follow. "This poor girl is terrified. I can sense it. The vials were put together very well. Why didn't she let us help her sooner?"

I remained quiet. The nausea and sweats were getting worse with each inch we rolled down the gravel drive. It felt as though a cold, clammy fog had seeped deep into my body, all the way to the bone, until even the slightest movement made me want to vomit.

"That's the place," I said, feeling dry heaves race up my throat. I pointed to the little trailer with all the bottles around it. The curtains were drawn, and the car I had seen Brit pull up in was parked next to it. The broom was also lying across the threshold.

"You wait here." Aunt Astrid, who normally maneuvered slowly and purposefully, picking her way through simultaneous dimensions, was walking quickly and nervously, like someone who was late for an appointment.

I nodded and kept my eyes open in little slits, hoping nothing would ambush us. I was in no condition to fight off a mosquito, let alone an attack from anyone.

If I closed my eyes, the entire world tipped over, flipping me violently around like a ping-pong ball on ocean waves. But when I opened my eyes, everything spun quickly, as if the Earth's rotation had sped up a thousand times its normal speed. If I even slightly turned my head, I was afraid I'd heave all over the inside of my car.

Looking around suspiciously, Aunt Astrid waved her arms. Within an instant, a floral-patterned sheet and a tattered pink towel flew like exotic birds from a neighbor's clothesline and gently landed over the vials on the stairs. The little jars sat all around the trailer, but covering just those few made a big enough difference that I was at least able to open my eyes.

Without hesitation, Aunt Astrid picked up the broom and tossed it over the stairs. The broom must have done something to her hand because I could see her shaking it and rubbing it against the back of her skirt as she knocked on the door with her other hand.

When the door opened, I could hear Brit yell. "Oh, no! Does she have her cat?"

My aunt tried to settle Brit down, but the girl shook off my aunt's gesture and continued to cuss and shout. "You've got ten seconds to get off my property before I call the police!"

I rolled my eyes. Our visit was not going well.

"No!" Brit said. As Aunt Astrid calmly talked to her in a low voice, I could hear her say "no" again. A "yes" that was much quieter. A "maybe." An "I don't think so."

Finally, I heard the mumbling of a halfway civil conversation. Aunt Astrid said something quiet to calm her down that I couldn't make out, and after a few seconds, Aunt Astrid waved for me to come up to the trailer.

I climbed out of the car, still feeling nauseated as I inched my way up the wooden steps to the front door.

After following my aunt inside, I closed the door tightly behind me. Brit walked past me, slipping the chain lock into place then peeking outside as if she were expecting to see someone else peering back at her.

I took a deep breath. The place smelled like vanilla, and I noticed two little votive candles burning on either side of a picture. The photograph was that of a very young Marvin Clegg and the young woman who had been his wife. The picture was lovely, and I would remember it later, but at the moment, the sickeningly sweet smell of the candles was making my stomach fold over onto itself.

"Can I offer you guys some coffee or maybe a

glass of water?" Brit sounded much calmer, nicer, to my surprise. Aunt Astrid could work wonders on people.

"I'd like water," I said, shocked at the weakness of my own voice.

My Aunt Astrid looked at me sternly as if to say, "Just hold on."

We were there to get information then get out. It seemed odd that my aunt had focused on me as if she had just seen me. I had never seen that look from her, and it was a little unnerving, like seeing someone who'd had long hair all her life suddenly show up with her head shaved... still the same person yet not.

Brit went into the little kitchenette, grabbed a bottle of water from her fridge, and quickly handed it to me.

Twisting off the cap, I took a quick, cold sip and felt a little better. Holding the cold bottle to my fore-head, I followed them into the sitting area.

"Are you all right?" Brit asked, looking me up and down with what I could only perceive as reluctant concern.

"Yeah, um... I think it was just something I ate. I'll be fine." I tried to brighten, smiling and nodding as I spoke.

"Brit, we don't want to take up too much of your time but... well, we need your help," Aunt Astrid said.

"I can't help you." Brit sat down on the edge of a rose-colored recliner. She looked around at the windows, stood, peeked out between them, then pulled the curtains tightly shut. She took her seat again on the edge of the chair.

"What are you looking for?" Aunt Astrid asked. "Are you expecting someone?"

Brit looked at us as if we had lobsters coming out of our ears. "Don't pretend you don't know she's out there."

"Who?" Aunt Astrid asked.

"Look, you said you needed to tell me something important. You said it had to do with my father and that you knew his heart attack wasn't... natural."

"You're afraid of something, Brit. Please, tell us what, or who?" My aunt took a seat on the edge of the couch closest to Brit and stretched out her hand to touch Brit's gently.

Brit swallowed, and tears filled her eyes. She stood up and walked to the door. For a second, I was sure she was going to rip off the chain, yank it open, and tell us not to let it hit us on our backsides on the way out. But she didn't. She peeked out the peephole then turned to face us, rubbing her hands together.

"She's constantly loitering around, and if it isn't her, it's her disgusting toady." Brit's voice was a harsh whisper. "I tried to like her. I tried to be nice to her, but something is wrong. Really wrong." Brit tapped her temple, her voice still low and raspy.

Aunt Astrid straightened her back and spoke low but confidently. "Brit, my daughter Bea's husband works for the police department. He's a detective and was at your father's house after you had called for help."

"Was he the really good-looking guy? Detective Samberg?" Brit asked, her eyes tired but twinkling a little.

I couldn't help but cough as a little water went down the wrong pipe when she mentioned Samberg as the really good-looking guy. I suppose Blake could be kind of handsome, in a brooding, pensive sort of way. He had the ability to look at a person and make them feel as if they were the only person in the room, and that could be quite terrifying if you were being interrogated for murder.

"No. Detective Jake Williams," Aunt Astrid said.

Brit nodded but didn't say anything more.

"Brit, he said he saw writing on the walls, symbols and weird letters. His gut told him there was more to the story than you were letting on. But he didn't have any proof, so the case was ruled natural causes and closed. But it wasn't natural, was it, Brit?"

Her eyes filled with tears. She shook her head.

"Can you tell us what you think is going on? Who did you try to be nice to?" I asked, my curiosity overcoming the nausea.

"That writing isn't on the walls anymore." Brit looked down at the carpet as if she were seeing her father's house in her mind. "It fades away. I don't know what it says. I think she just does it to mess with people."

"Who?" I was nearly begging. I wanted a name and preferably an address, then I wanted to get out of there and start feeling better. Aunt Astrid seemed totally unfazed.

Brit crossed the room, pulled back the long, heavy curtains, and peeked out the sliding glass door. I noticed a line of white along the floor. She had poured salt there.

"This is what I do. I don't have any schedule because she'll see me, and I don't want her to know

I'll be at any certain place at any certain time. So every day is different. Every day is confusing and messy. I can't even get into the house I grew up in to tie up the loose ends because she'll eventually come by."

Wiping her eyes as she spoke, Brit seemed to have transformed from the woman who stole my cat into a girl who was alone in the world.

Aunt Astrid produced a beautiful lace handkerchief from her purse and handed it to Brit.

"This is so pretty." Brit said with a little smile. "I don't want to ruin it."

She tried to hand it back, but my aunt shook her head. "It's okay, honey. I've got hundreds of them."

Whatever was in those eight words was enough to break the wall Brit had built around herself. She broke down and sobbed.

"I miss him so much. I didn't even get a chance to say goodbye. It didn't have to happen. She did this. I don't care what the police say, or what the funeral home says, or what you people say! She killed him! And now, she's coming after me! And I'm all alone!"

Aunt Astrid pursed her lips together and took hold of Brit's hand. "You are not alone, Brit. Please, tell me her name."

Brit looked at Aunt Astrid then at me as if she suddenly realized we were in the room. Swallowing hard, she spoke barely over a whisper. "Jennifer Skala. That is her name."

High Priestess

Neither my aunt nor myself had heard the woman's name before.

"My father said he knew her from years back before he met my mother," Brit said. "He said they had gone on a couple of dates, but that she was always a little too clingy, you know? The kind of girl who always had to be told she was pretty. We've all met that kind."

Images of Darla Castellan flipping her hair at the café and getting that poor schmuck she'd just met to carry her bags popped into my head. Yes, Brit. We had all met that kind. I felt my stomach grind over on itself at the thought of my own high school nemesis.

"So, she showed up again at my school a few

years after my mother had passed away. She came up to me and asked if I was Marvin Clegg's daughter. She made it sound like they had kept in touch over the years. I talked with her on the phone. I went to lunch with her. She told me about places she had gone and things she had done and that she was a high priestess in some Wiccan group. I don't know. I just laughed it off." Brit wiped her nose and stared at the carpet.

"What did your father do when you told him you were talking with her?" I asked.

Brit chewed her bottom lip. "He didn't seem to mind at first. He told me she was a little on the crazy side when he knew her, but that she had probably mellowed by now. I liked her, sort of. We'd go shopping sometimes, and she'd ask me all about him. When I look back on it, I don't know why I didn't see it before. But she was really intrusive, you know?"

Still sweating and hoping my stomach would hold still if I did, I slowly leaned in a little closer as Brit continued her tale.

"She wanted to know if my father was dating. She wanted to know if I thought he'd like her to visit. And she was always asking me to tell him stuff like she had her boobs done and that she wasn't seeing anyone and had never been married. How could I have missed all this? I just repeated it all to my father like a parrot. I don't even know what I was hoping for. I didn't want my father to date this woman. But yet, I kept doing what she said."

"It's not your fault, Brit. Some people can be very persuasive, manipulative," Aunt Astrid said seriously. "Good-hearted people often have to learn the hard way how to spot these kinds of people." My aunt's face was getting angrier by the minute from the story she was hearing.

"Well, I decided to stop talking to her when I caught her with Lucas."

"Who is that?" I murmured, quickly sipping a little more water.

"I don't know what their official story is, but not long after I started communicating with Jennifer on a regular basis, I saw this guy with her all the time. He was a weird, gothic dude in his late forties. Too old to be wearing eyeliner, that's for sure. How cliché."

I rolled my eyes, thinking the exact same thing.

"He started coming with us to lunch or shopping. It was just plain creepy. Sometimes, when he thought I wasn't looking, I'd catch him staring at me. He looked at me like I was a steak on a platter." Brit shivered as she spoke.

"Did he speak to you?" I asked.

"No." Brit straightened up in her chair. "He'd mumble and whisper things to Jennifer but never directly to me. I thought... and this is totally gross, but I thought they were swingers or something and were sizing my dad up for something weird. Now, I only wish they were just pervy instead of..." She started to cry again.

"What happened between her and your father?" Aunt Astrid asked, trying to keep Brit going with her story.

"Jennifer showed up at my apartment by the school. I had never given her my address. I always met her somewhere. She had my phone number, but that was all. And she started calling me first thing when I got up and a couple times a night after I got home from school and work. When she showed up all dressed in black, with bright red nails and lipstick, and her hair all wild and hanging down her back, I told her no way. She looked ridiculous. Like she was dressed up for Halloween a couple months early. And Lucas was just as bad. I honestly didn't want to be seen with them."

Brit stood and peeked out the peephole of her front door.

"Jennifer said it was time she paid my father a

visit. That she had been wanting to see him for such a long time. That he was this great guy she never forgot. Blah, blah, blah. I told her to do what she wanted. I was getting tired of her. She begged me to go with her to see him, but I said no." As Brit sat back down again, she clenched her hands into fists. Her voice dropped to an angry drone. "That was when she told me she wasn't just a Wiccan high priestess. She started going on and on about being some divine messenger, untouchable, a super-powerful, centuries-old witch. It was just crazy talk."

"Oh, Brit, you poor thing." My aunt was very upset. Those kinds of people were horrors to her because the Greenstones worked so hard to dispel that kind of thinking.

"She told me that my father and I had been chosen to be her new family. And we'd be powerful and feared and all this other crazy stuff that I couldn't believe I was hearing. Who talks like this?"

I shook my head in disbelief.

"So I told her that sounded insane, but if she wanted to see my father, I couldn't stop her. So off she went in her Elvira Mistress of the Night gown and tacky jewelry with Lucas strutting along behind her like the guy who scoops poop up behind an elephant in those old cartoons."

Despite my queasiness, I let out a chuckle.

"You know what I'm talking about?" Brit asked, looking at me with the first sign of joy I'd seen on her face since we met. I nodded, and even she had to chuckle.

"Of course, I called my dad to warn him," she continued. "He said not to worry, and that he'd deal with her. He said she was always a little weird. He told me that part of the reason he couldn't continue dating her was that aside from her insane insecurities, she started playing with Ouija boards, reading all kinds of stuff on the occult. I mean, if you knew my dad, you'd know this wasn't his style."

Brit's eyes shot to her father's picture on the little altar with the burning vanilla votive candles. "We're just plain people. He went to church. He liked to play solitaire and watch old cowboy movies and make candy. That was about it. Nothing fancy. Nothing weird. He was just my dad. And when he shot her down, when he refused her... she went insane."

"When did this happen? When did she go and see your father for the first time?" I asked, wishing I could just go outside and kick all those vials far away from me.

"Maybe six months ago. From then on, she kept

driving by his house. She'd leave notes at his door, but when my dad would try and show them to me, the writing would disappear right in front of us. He said he'd seen her parked across the street from the candy store. She'd peek at him around corners if he were grocery shopping or going for coffee. I told him I didn't like any of it, but he said it was just to get attention. If he ignored her long enough, he thought she'd get bored and leave."

"But she never did," my aunt said.

Brit shook her head. "It made her madder. One time, I came home from school to stay with Dad for the weekend and found her sneaking around my father's house. She was putting weird dried things around and strange trinkets and crystals. When I looked it up online, I found out that those things were supposed to start a fire if a person said some kind of chant. I told my dad, but he said he didn't believe in that stuff, so it couldn't hurt him."

"What did she do when she saw you?" I asked, wiping sweat from my forehead.

"She looked at me and walked slowly back to her car then sped off." Brit took a deep breath. "I should have called the cops so there would at least be a record. But Dad said no. Then I saw her doing the same kind of thing around his shop. When I stayed overnight at my dad's house, which became more and more frequent, I'd hear things outside. I'd hear footsteps and mumbling and laughing. And then the cats started to show up."

"Is that why you took Treacle?" I asked.

"Treacle? Is that your cat's name? That's pretty. I was calling him kitty when I had him." She looked up at me as if she were ashamed of herself. "I am so sorry about that. I love animals. I do. But with her doing all the things she was doing, claiming to be a witch or priestess or whatever she thought she was, I started doing some research and, well, a black cat can be a lucky talisman for someone like me. It can also be quite a power shot for someone like her. Because I believe she is a witch. You can go ahead and think I'm crazy but..."

With trembling hands, Brit pulled her hair away from her face and let out a deep sigh. "Jennifer Skala is evil. She's got a blackness around her, and she's made friends with it. I've seen it. It peeks at me from around corners and knocks on my door and rattles the windows at night. It would at my father's house, too. That was why I was looking at getting him into a community. I thought with people around, cameras, a security guard, and a few trinkets planted around, I could keep him safe. It was a long shot, but

I was desperate. I just wanted the old man safe, you know? Turns out he had nowhere to run to even if he did want to go."

It seemed as if getting this story out, even to two relative strangers, was helping Brit. She leaned back in her chair. "So the cats started showing up. They'd stare at the house and watch my father and I as we came and went. They'd be sitting outside the candy shop. They'd be at the library. They'd show up if we went to McDonald's or did the grocery shopping. They'd show up here and stare at the trailer. Sometimes, they'd howl and fight. Have you ever heard cats fighting? It's a very unnerving sound. The things were everywhere, and the saddest part was I don't think they wanted to be doing what they were doing."

"What makes you say that?" Aunt Astrid asked before I could.

"Normal cats study people. These cats seemed to have a begging quality behind their eyes. Such independent animals should never be forced to sit still. And that's what she was making them do. I believe she was making them do this. Jeez, I sound like I'm off my rocker, but it's true.

"The cats kept showing up, and they'd get skinnier and skinnier, like whatever she was doing didn't allow them to eat. Then one day, one of them would be gone, and another one would have taken its place until it got too skinny and disappeared. And sometimes, I'd see Jennifer peeking around the other trailers, staring at the black cat. Your Treacle.

"I would be inside, scared to death that she'd come break in. She'd talk to herself or to Lucas, saying things like 'I want that cat' or 'that cat will be mine.' Every couple of days, once she knew I had him, she was sneaking around. I don't know if the vials really work, or if she's just cowardly, but after I put them out and poured salt, she had to keep her distance. That was all after my father died. My father who never had a health problem in his life dies of a sudden heart attack."

"Where is your bathroom?" I asked desperately. I'd like to say I held my own and just needed to splash some cold water on my face.

Brit pointed behind her, and I dashed off, slamming the door behind me. The power of the witches' vials, compounded by Brit's tale, was getting to me. The horrible abuse being inflicted on cats—the creatures witches considered valuable and powerful companions— was too much for me to bear.

I'm not sure how long I was in the bathroom. My mind kept saying 'get up, they're waiting for you,' but my body said 'don't try to move, or you'll regret it.' I moved. I regretted it. But I managed to pull the door open and step back into the living room.

My aunt stood up and came to me. "You poor dear," she whispered, pushing my hair away from my sweaty face. "We're almost done." She turned to Brit, who was also standing and wringing her hands nervously.

"Brit, do you have any idea where Jennifer is staying?" Aunt Astrid asked.

She shook her head. Suddenly, her eyes popped wide. "No, I don't know where she's staying, but I've got a picture of her I can show you. I took it on my phone just so she'd know I saw her. I also read I might be able to stop her by using a picture and a spell and, well... it can't hurt, right?" She pulled her phone from her pocket and showed us the picture.

"If she's sneaking around," I said with slightly slurred words, "why haven't you told the police?"

Brit rolled her eyes. "What would I tell them? This woman says she's a witch? She killed my dad with her witchy powers, and now she's after me?"

Aunt Astrid shook her head then took Brit's hands. "You have no idea how much you've helped us, Brit. Your father would be very proud of you."

Aunt Astrid hugged the girl then let go, took my hand, and began heading toward the door.

"I don't mean to be rude, but what do you guys think you can do against her?" Brit asked. "I think she *is* a witch. I think she can hurt people without touching them, and I think she likes doing it. I'd suggest getting some witches' vials and salt for your homes. Because if she didn't know you've been here before, she knows you've been here now."

"Oh, uh, like I said, my daughter's husband is a detective," my aunt said quickly. "We might be able to help."

Brit peeked through the peephole, and after deciding the coast was clear, opened the door. The cool night air felt great, and I inhaled it deeply.

"I am sorry I took your cat," Brit said. "But please, guard him with your life. At the risk of sounding even crazier, don't let her get her hands on him. She'll use him up and then kill him."

My body shivered at the thought. "I won't. I promise." I hobbled weakly down the wooden steps. Before I could turn around, Brit had the door closed, and I heard the lock slip back into place.

"Do you need me to drive?" my aunt asked as I limped pitifully to the car.

"No. No. I can do it. You better uncover her jars.

From the sound of it, she needs them. They work quite well... at least, on me they do. They didn't seem to have any effect on you."

My aunt waved her arms and sent the sheet and towel back to their places on the neighbor's clothesline. Once both of us were in the car, she spoke. "I couldn't see."

"What?" I gasped. "What are you talking about?"

"I couldn't see, couldn't see a thing but a few shadows and shapes moving around the room. Those vials took away my vision. I couldn't see the past, the future, another dimension, or even this one."

"You sounded different." My legs felt stronger as we drove away, but my head was pounding.

"It was the first time in my life that I didn't see a dozen things taking place at the same time. The first time I was almost like everyone else. I enjoyed it. The simplicity of it." She turned her head and smiled at me.

"Well, it made me puke, literally. I didn't enjoy it."

Aunt Astrid patted my arm, and as we got to the road that led back to Bea's place, we were both feeling much better. But Bea had been correct—the psychic backwash we were going to swallow was going to be hell to pay tomorrow.

Walona Motel

꧁꧂

As soon as I pulled the car into Bea's driveway, she came running out of the house, slamming the door shut behind her. She was waving and shouting, and her eyes were wild. My first thought was that something had happened to Jake or Blake.

"You won't believe this!" she called before the car was even in park. "Hurry! Hurry!"

"What?" I asked, a little annoyed due to my upset tummy.

"Jake called."

"Yeah, and?" I got out of the car and slowly walked toward the house with Aunt Astrid at my side.

"He reported to a scene at the Walona Motel."

"Eww, gross. He was just over there the other day. That place right by the expressway, right? Do I want to hear this? The Walona isn't exactly known for high-profile celebrity clientele, I hear."

"Right?" Bea nodded in agreement. "But Jake said there was a woman there answering questions about the noises she'd heard in the room next to hers. Apparently, the man there was dealing with some shady people, had a big argument, and then bingo—this woman said he had a heart attack."

"So? Maybe this person just had a good old-fashioned heart attack," I said with about as much tact as a porcupine in a room full of balloons.

"And what makes her so special that Jake had to call you?" Aunt Astrid asked.

"He thought that he was being funny when he said she was dressed all in black. She had this whole gothic theme going on, including wearing a pentagram in rhinestones on a big, gaudy ring. He wanted to know if I'd like him to introduce us, you know, like a joke. If we wanted to add anyone to the coven, are his exact words. He thinks he's so clever. I told him... Cath, what's the matter?"

My heart stopped beating, and for a split second, I thought I was going to have a heart attack myself.

"Did you say a ring with a rhinestone pentagram on it?"

Bea repeated herself and described the woman as Jake told her. Aunt Astrid and I agreed that it had to be the woman Brit had shown us a picture of, complete with that ring of horror and tackiness from my dream.

Quickly, I told them about my dream—the fog and the thing crawling through my window just before I snapped awake—and how it came true, with the threatening notices, the cats that started showing up, and all that other witchy business.

"Did she give the woman's name?" I asked.

"Yes, Jennifer something, I don't remember."

Close enough. I was feeling as though we had her trapped. It would take just a day or two, maybe just a matter of hours, before we would have her cornered and begging to go to jail. She would wish she didn't even know how to spell the word *witch*, let alone pretend to be one.

"So, who was the man?"

"She said she just met him at the motel when she checked in. She was in town visiting friends. She said she didn't know what he was doing there. Living there, perhaps. But she felt sorry for him since he was all alone."

"She sounds very charitable," I said sarcastically.

"Yeah, well, Jake said she was coming on strong with him even as the ambulance was wheeling away her neighbor under a white sheet on a stretcher. You don't act that way when death is that close to you."

And you don't act that way with Bea's husband, I thought.

"Lucas. That was the guy's name. I don't know if that was his first or last name, but that was what I heard Jake say to Detective Samberg before he hung up the phone with me."

"So we've got her." I rubbed my stomach to try to help the queasiness out of my system. Bea nodded with excitement.

"Not quite, girls," Aunt Astrid said as we made our way to Bea's kitchen. My aunt took her seat on the stool at the end of the counter. "Yes, in the world of witches, she has committed horrible crimes against the universe. But in Wonder Falls, she hasn't done a thing. Nothing that could be pinned on her at any rate." She pointed to the kettle, letting Bea know she wanted some tea.

I grabbed a step stool and pulled down the Doritos from their hiding place that Jake had revealed earlier. But one whiff of the processed cheesy goodness made me weak in the knees and light-headed. I put them back, swallowed hard, and pulled up a stool next to my aunt.

"Maybe we should sleep on it." Bea yawned. "It's already past ten o'clock, and we still have to work in the morning."

"I think that's a good idea," Aunt Astrid said, still pointing at the cold, empty kettle while looking at Bea.

"Oh, you want some tea, Mom? Is that it?" Bea rolled her eyes and smiled, snatching the teapot and quickly filling it from the tap. "It's not like you don't know how to make tea," she teased.

"It just tastes better when you do it." They both laughed.

I was sure Bea's tea would sooth my stomach, but the thought of trying to get it down was too much. I just wanted to go home and sleep in my own bed.

"Are you sure you think it's safe? We've got lots of room and love having everyone around," Bea said.

"Yeah, I'm sure. That trip to Brit's really knocked me out, and I think I'd really just like to be around my own things. Plus, I have the feeling I may be up and down a couple times during the night. The last thing I want is an audience."

I looked at Treacle who was sitting up straight,

looking out the back door. His eyes were little green slits, but I knew he wasn't sleeping. He was studying.

"I think you should stay here," I said to him in my mind. *"You're safer here than with me."* I walked over to him when he didn't respond. *"Treacle? Are you all right?"* Stooping over, I felt the world spin again but picked the big furry ball up in my arms. He let out a little growl like he used to when he was a kitten and watching a bird hop near the windowsill... as if he were trying to coax it closer and closer until he could catch it.

"Something is out there," he thought to me.

I held him close and looked out into the darkness. *"Are you sure?"*

"Yes. But whatever it is, it can't get closer. It has a weakness, and it can't get closer."

"Is it another cat?"

"No. It's what the cats see for."

I stood there, rocking the cat in my arms, letting the heat from his body soothe my aching belly. I strained to see some kind of movement, some ghoulish face, or a pair of eyes blinking back at me, but all I saw was darkness.

"We will take care of him," Peanut Butter said,

wrapping his body around my leg and standing bravely at the door, looking out.

"Yes, we have a plan of our own should anything find its way in," Marshmallow said, prancing up to Peanut Butter and nudging him gently with her head.

"Don't you guys take any risks. If anything happens, run and hide," I said to them.

"Run and hide. Only after we teach whatever that is out there a lesson that you don't mess with our family." Peanut Butter quickly licked his front paw then resumed his vigil.

I contemplated telling them about what Brit had said about this woman's abusive treatment of cats. I don't know what she could have done to get inside their heads, to control them so cruelly, as though they were replaceable tools to be thrown away when she was done with them. I didn't. I couldn't bring myself to tell them. *"This thing is dangerous. Just do me a favor, and don't take any chances. Okay?"*

They all looked up at me and meowed in unison.

Meteor Showers

✦

As I drove, I began to feel as though I really wanted to talk to someone about anything but witchcraft. It was late, but I wondered if Min was around. I decided to drive past his parent's house and see if his car was in the driveway.

As the familiar roads wound and weaved around, I let out a big sigh. My stomach was starting to feel better. I thought of a double cheeseburger and didn't feel the need to pull over and gag.

I knew Treacle was unhappy but safe for the time being. My blood boiled to think of that woman torturing cats. Even the alley cats had their own ways of doing things. Her treatment was cruel, like slave labor.

So, this Jennifer person was a woman scorned, as

if none of us had ever had our hearts broken before. I hated to admit it, but I thought of Min and Amalia. It would have been easier if she were a crackpot, but she wasn't. She was probably more normal than me, and I consider myself a pretty down-to-earth person, with a few extra talents no one can ever know about.

I was seriously starting to depress myself when I looked in my rearview mirror and noticed the guy behind me had his high beams on.

"Jeez, thanks, pal. I don't have a bad *enough* headache," I grumbled, flipping the mirror to tint in an attempt to tone down the brightness.

I turned off down a side street that was home to some of the wealthier people who lived in Wonder Falls. Darla lived in a mansion high up on a hill around there, but it was easy to avoid. I decided to do just that.

These were homes for families. I wouldn't know what to do with so much space, but it sure would be an awesome challenge to imagine. As I looked through some of the open windows, I saw beautifully decorated rooms painted in rich reds or browns. It seemed as if the people knew exactly where to put everything to make it look beautiful.

And speaking of beautiful, I wondered what Brit meant about Blake being the really good-looking detective. Jake had always been what most women thought of as a tall glass of water. I didn't think anyone but me thought Blake was the better-looking one, not that I thought he was hot or anything. But he had some pleasing features I liked. If he would keep his mouth closed, he would be perfect. Maybe. What was I thinking? It certainly wasn't the time or place to be considering the positive attributes of Blake Samberg.

How were we ever going to get to Jennifer before she got to Brit, Bea, Aunt Astrid, and myself... and anyone else who looked at her cock-eyed? I wanted to just cruise along, but the guy driving behind me was in some kind of hurry, tailgating and weaving back and forth. I hit my hazard lights and pulled over to let him pass.

"Leave five minutes early if you don't want to be late," I mumbled as I looked in the rearview mirror. The car pulled slowly around mine. It was dark outside, but as I looked at the driver, something very unsettling looked back at me.

Suddenly, I felt like the locked car door and rolled-up window may not be enough protection for me. I could make out a silhouette by the glow of the streetlamps. It had long, wild hair, a grin like a starving animal, and white eyes.

It was her. Jennifer Skala knew where I'd come from and was passing me slowly on the street. I could feel her evil presence like you'd smell garbage from the opening of an alley. You knew it was deep in there and that it was foul without getting anywhere near it.

She drove past then suddenly hit the gas, speeding off just far enough to turn around. She flashed her lights and revved the engine. Was she seriously going to ram me?

The thing about us witches is that we could be killed by regular, good old-fashioned car accidents, too. I couldn't tell what this lunatic was thinking, but she was ready to push the envelope. She hit the gas, and her car burst to life, zooming straight for me.

I put my arms up, unable to move quickly enough to do much more, and squeezed my eyes shut. Nothing... no shattering impact, no sound of crunching metal, no glass breaking. Letting out the breath I hadn't even realized I was holding, I opened one eye and peeked around. I was alone on the street. Shifting quickly in my seat, I turned around.

Maybe she'd passed me. Maybe at the last second, her car had swerved, and I'd see her taillights getting smaller and smaller as she drove away.

But there were no red taillights. No other car was on the street. I was completely alone.

"This is ridiculous," I grumbled, putting the car in gear and pulling back onto the road.

Min's house was only a few blocks away. I hoped he was there and the lights were still on. It was almost eleven o'clock—a little late to be calling, but as I rounded the corner of his street, I was happy to see his car. In fact, I was really happy because he was standing right by his car... and so was Amalia.

"Oh, geez," I groaned. How was this going to look? "Hi, Min. I know it's late, but I just happened to be in the neighborhood and thought I'd see if you had a shoulder to lean on right now." Yikes. That sounded like something out of a cheesy Lifetime movie about torrid affairs or deadly marriages.

Min and Amalia both looked up at the same time and saw me. I flashed my lights as I pulled my car to the curb and cut the engine.

"Cath! What a nice surprise!" Min smiled broadly.

"Hey, Min," I said as casually as I could. "Hi, Amalia. I hope I'm not interrupting anything."

"Cath!" Amalia almost ran up to me. "No. My gosh, it's so nice to see you. You know, Min and I were just hanging out here because he said there was a meteor shower tonight, but I could have sworn it was next week."

"Yeah, I heard about that. Sorry, Min, but the lady is correct. That is *next* week." I had almost forgotten about the meteor shower coming up. If we didn't get that lunatic Jennifer Skala in line before then, heaven only knew what she might do.

When the heavens moved through their celestial routine, us witches would experience varying degrees of power. Sometimes, our powers were stronger than other times. Meteor showers were like spontaneous bursts of energy. They were fun and exciting, enhancing our gifts and sometimes enlightening us to a new power, temporary or permanent. It was all up to the heavens.

"Oh well, you can't blame a guy for trying." He smiled down at Amalia. "So, what are you doing around here at this hour, Cath? Not that we'd ever mind a visit from you any time day or night."

"I didn't mean to break up your little stargazing party. Actually, I started to get a little dizzy as I was driving and thought I should pull over for a spell." It wasn't a complete lie. I didn't have any reason to mention the witches' vials at Brit's place that made me sicker than a dog or the phantom driver, who tailgated me then proceeded to drive directly into my headlights only to disappear a split second before impact.

"You do look a little pale, Cath," Amalia said. Grabbing me by the wrist, she gave me a puzzled look. "My gosh, girl, your heart is pumping to beat the band. Come on and have a seat on the porch."

"I'll get you some water." Min dashed into the house.

"I'm really all right. Just something I ate, I think." That excuse worked before.

"You know, you don't want to be driving in traffic and feel the urge to puke, pardon my French. I had that happen to me once," Amalia said in one quick breath of air. She pulled up a small cushioned ottoman and sat down next to me. "There was a twenty-four hour flu going around the Home. It had worked its way through every patient and every nurse on staff within two weeks. I was feeling good, thinking all the orange juice and exercise I was doing had my antibodies in better shape than the rest of them."

I watched Amalia as she told her story, polishing her nails on her chest as she spoke, then rolling her eyes and shaking her head in disgust as she continued.

"I'm on my way home, traffic is moving but packed, and it hits me."

"Oh, no," I said, completely engrossed in her tale.

"Yup. I started to sweat, felt nauseated, and before I could put on my blinker to pull to the right, my whole dashboard… well, let's just say, it wasn't pretty."

I couldn't help it. I started to laugh.

"And if that isn't bad enough, home was still twenty-five minutes away."

Then I was really chuckling.

"The worst part is…"

"You mean that wasn't the worst part?" I laughed some more as Amalia started to laugh with me.

"No. The worst part was that my car was in the shop. This was my sister's car."

"Well, if you're an optimist, then perhaps that was the best part," I said, gasping for breath as I laughed.

"I never thought of it like that. I was too busy feeling awful all these years when I should have been thrilled."

By the time Min came out with a glass of water garnished with a delicate slice of lemon, I was not only feeling a world of better, but I was still laughing with Amalia.

A Thug

※

I didn't stay for very long, maybe a half an hour... forty-five minutes tops. Min and Amalia would never know how much good they did for me.

I listened to them tell stories about their day, and Amalia was like an open book. The poor thing was more than happy to laugh at what seemed to be a never-ending series of unfortunate events.

On her day off about three months ago, she managed to put gas in her car, drop off dry cleaning, and make it halfway through grocery shopping before someone told her that her skirt was tucked into her pantyhose.

At work, one of the new residents had received flowers from her family, and when Amalia went to fill up a vase, she spilled all the water on her shirt. Nursing uniforms are quite sturdy, built to stand up to all kinds of spills, and hers was no different. Ironically, the uniform had multicolored cats all over it. When she got home and took off her shirt, the colors of the cats had transferred onto her skin.

"I looked like I had Morgellons disease. All these goofy, multicolored lines all over me. It took over a week of near-scalding hot baths to get them off completely."

The way she told a story had me in stitches. I found myself liking her more and more. It wasn't just because she was so willing to share her misfortune with a smile and such good nature, but I saw a lot of myself in her.

She never talked about going out with girlfriends or partying or anything like that. She worked and kept to herself until Min came along... just as he'd done for me in high school.

When I finally left, I felt good. For the first time in a couple of days, I felt like myself. A good night's sleep in my own bed, knowing my cat and family were safe, was all I needed. But as I drove down the dark and deserted streets, I began to feel uneasy.

I couldn't be sure, but I thought every couple of blocks, I saw the glowing eyes of felines peering out at me from the roadside, from around mailboxes, from side streets and alleyways. I scanned the roads for any other cars but saw none.

Finally, I arrived at my house. I swear that the journey, which had only taken about ten minutes, felt like it had slowed down. I was shocked to see it was only a little after midnight. I had been sure it was at least two in the morning.

Climbing out of my car, I listened and heard nothing. As I walked up the steps to my house, my footsteps echoed loudly. The key slipping into the lock sounded like an explosion against the quiet neighborhood. Again, I listened but heard nothing. Shrugging, I slipped inside, locked the door behind me, and let out my breath.

Without Treacle, the house was very still. Just to be on the safe side, I checked all the windows and the back door and found everything to be locked up tight, just as I had left it.

Even though Bea's home was spacious and lovely and always smelled of a soothing spice or flower, I loved being in my own little house. Sage hung in the air, my crystals hung from the corners of the ceiling, and my clothes, notes, magazines, and books were scattered wherever I set them. Even the most skilled witch should appreciate her own sacred space.

Letting the water heat up in my shower, I thought of Amalia's story and began to chuckle again. The shower felt good and helped clear my mind. When I finally emerged, my fingers were prunes and my internal temperature was raised, so the cool air outside the bathroom felt invigorating. Slipping into flannel pajamas, I checked all the doors and windows again, left one light on in the living room, crawled into bed, and snapped off the light on the nightstand.

Then it hit me. There was no sound outside. No sound of any kind. No crickets. No hum from the busy streets a couple of blocks down. There was no wind rustling the leaves.

My eyes popped wide open, and I held my breath.

"Meow-er-eow!"

A layer of sweat instantly broke out all over me. Not wanting to look but feeling an invisible pull turn my head, I turned to the window and saw not just one but three sets of glowing eyes staring in at me from behind a tiny slit of open curtain.

The cats banged and scratched viciously at the window with a feverish determination. What they would have done to me had they been able to get in, I don't know. But I saw nothing in those glowing orbs that would make me think they were anything other than fully consumed by the beast that had chosen them to do her dirty work.

I got out of bed carefully and looked at them. I tried to talk to them, to hear their thoughts, but I couldn't. All I could hear was screaming.

PING! PING! PING! The light, bouncy sound of my cell phone ringing made me jump and clutch my chest.

I walked over to the phone, expecting it to be my aunt or Bea calling to tell me it was like a crazy cat lady's dream come true at their house, with a couple of dozen felines howling and meowing in their yard.

Instead, when I answered, I felt an ice-cold breath across the back of my neck.

"Cath? Why do they call you that? You have half a name because you are just half a person. They all know that. Don't you?" The voice on the other end of the phone was hypnotic. I began to tremble, but I couldn't put the phone down. "I can see you." Her sing-songy voice reminded me of the condescending way Darla used to insult me in high school, with her voice sounding kind, even though the words were anything but. "Did you like my driving tonight? You looked like you did."

"What do you want?" I managed to squeak, angry with myself for not sounding tougher.

"You know what I want. I want your cat." She sounded frustrated. "You don't even know what he's capable of doing. You have no idea what kind of power he could radiate because you just want him as a pet. A companion because you don't have a man."

"You can't have him."

"Oh, says you?"

"Yeah."

"You know, Cath, you might know who I am now, but you don't know what I am."

"I know what you *think* you are. You think you're some kind of witch. It takes a little more than black clothes and a bedazzled pentagram to make a witch."

The other end of the phone was quiet for a moment. I was hoping she was embarrassed over that tacky ring.

"I'm not just a witch. Brit's little trinkets won't be able to stop me once I have the power of your black cat at my disposal. Don't worry, once he's mine he'll probably forget all about you."

"It'll be over my dead body before you get my cat," I growled into the phone, wishing I could reach through the line and strangle her. Especially when she laughed at me.

"That sounds about right. And the beautiful thing is I can do it. To you. To that old hippie. To the one married to that handsome detective who would inevitably need a shoulder to cry on… or more."

"You're disgusting. You're a slob. We've seen your work. You got lucky a couple of times, that's it. Anyone could make a mess like you did. You're a hack." When I genuinely laughed at Jennifer, she said nothing. "I'll tell you what, Jennifer, if you knew anything, you might have tried a love spell on Marvin to get him to notice your softer side. But see, you didn't even have the smarts to do that. You just resort to violence. Like a thug. Like an ignorant thug."

"I'll show you a…"

"You won't show me anything. Oh, I take that back. You'll show me a bunch of cats who will do what? Scratch my furniture until I beg for mercy?" A surge of positive energy coursed through me. I suddenly realized what was happening. Jennifer, having chosen to learn from those darker shadows and beasts in other dimensions, could not maintain the upper hand for long if her victim wasn't afraid. My gosh, how terrified had Marvin been for her to do what she did to him? "Tell me, Jennifer, what was your plan for Lucas? Did he know you were just using him? Or did he…"

"Shut your mouth, subcreature!" she screamed

into the phone. Her voice was like a growl and a scream all at once.

I think I had just gone one step too far. "Yeah, okay. You're real tough over the phone, Jennifer, but how would you be if I was right in front of you? You think I'm scared of a voice? You think I'm scared of someone who has to stick to the shadows and uses cats because she's so horrible, she knows no one wants to even look at her?"

I was shaking as the words came out of me, especially when the other end of the line had gone silent.

Then I remembered something Jake had said about the notes we received. Jennifer could do parlor tricks. She could make cats act crazy to freak us out and deliver notes, but she was still using the things in this world for most of her scare tactics. And her psychic attacks were as chaotic as her own mind was. She was no match for the Greenstones.

"Jennifer, are you still there?"

"Your whole world is going to become very dark, very soon." Her voice was low and gravelly.

"Yeah, yeah, well, that may be. But let's just say we handle this like big witches. You meet me by the waterfall tomorrow at one in the morning. Do you know where that is? There's a clearing where the water begins to fall. It's out of the way. Quiet. No way for an ambush. And let's settle this. If you win, you get Treacle, and I'll step aside. If I win…"

"Deal," she said without listening to me, then the phone clicked and went dead.

I looked at the phone. The number was listed as unknown, which I thought was kind of creepy. But the decision I had made, this duel I had arranged, felt oddly comforting.

Until I remembered I had to tell Bea and Aunt Astrid.

Fight

✿

"Are you out of your mind?" Aunt Astrid asked me the next morning after we had opened the café. "How could you just challenge her to a duel without even discussing it with us?"

I stood with my hands thrust deep in my jeans pockets as if I were back in high school and being questioned about a failed exam. I shrugged, not looking up.

"She makes people's hearts explode!" Bea hissed so as not to be overheard by the patrons who were seated in the café, drinking. "Did you forget about that?"

"No, I didn't forget," I mumbled.

"Then what? What made you think this was a

good idea?" Aunt Astrid asked, not caring about the people who turned to look at her. "I lost my sister because she went into something unprepared. I don't plan on losing my niece the same way."

I looked up at my aunt. "What do you mean my mom wasn't prepared?" I asked quietly.

"Don't try and change the subject. You might be in your own house, paying your own way, but Cath, you are still my responsibility. You can't just assume you can handle anything thrown your way. Sometimes, you need to let the universe tell you what to do."

"I thought I was. I have a hunch. I have a gut feeling that meeting her up there is the answer."

"The answer to what?" Bea asked.

"The answer to getting her to stop."

Aunt Astrid looked at me gravely.

"Aunt Astrid." I leaned in to whisper in her ear. "Jennifer Skala is just a big bully. When you take away the gruesomeness, she's no different than a punk in school."

"I hope you're right."

"I think I am." I smiled weakly at both of them.

"Mom, there's got to be some kind of passage we can find to help with this," Bea said. "Somewhere in one of your books, there has got to be something that would help."

Aunt Astrid planted both hands on her hips and looked around the café. "If there is, I can't think of it offhand."

Bea scooted gracefully around the counter, wiping her hands on her apron. "Sorry, folks, family emergency. We're closing for the day."

A chorus of groans went up as chairs began scraping the floor. Papers rustled, and the bell behind the door jingled as the customers slowly exited.

"We're sorry. So Sorry. Some things just can't be helped. But come back tomorrow for a free coffee or tea and a slice of apple pie."

"What?" I asked. "They don't need to get a freebie for this, do they?"

"Compliments of my soul sister here. She'll be buying your coffee for you tomorrow. Thanks so much for understanding." Bea continued to usher people gently toward the door, winking at me as I felt my paycheck totally disappear before I'd even earned it.

I locked up the front door and flipped the CLOSED sign. We told Kevin he was welcome to go home, but he insisted on staying and getting a jump on those free pies we'd be giving away the next day. He said he'd be sure to lock up when he left.

"We need to get the cats," I said as everyone piled into my car. We drove to Bea's place, then all of us, each with a cat in her arms, got back in the car.

Treacle, who was usually quite at ease in the car, was trembling in my arms. *"Don't you hear it?"* he said to me. *"It's like someone keeps calling my name. I keep hearing it and wanting to go there, but…"*

"It's not what you think it is, Treacle." I looked at the other cats. *"Marshmallow, Peanut Butter, how are you guys feeling?"*

"We hear it, too." Marshmallow shifted in Aunt Astrid's arms. *"But it's not calling Treacle. It's calling me."*

"No," Peanut Butter said. *"It's me. I told you it was me. I heard it first."*

I felt the blood drain from my face. She was starting already. Jennifer was going to get to me by getting to my cat first. We had to find something to stop her.

I backed out of the driveway and quickly pulled onto the street. Before I'd gotten ten feet away from the house, I slammed on the brakes, causing everyone to lurch forward.

"Look! Over there!" I pointed to a long-haired

woman getting into a silver car and speeding away. She was wearing all black.

"Is that her?" Treacle asked.

"I'll bet it is," I said. *"We have to hurry. Who knows what she'll try to do to us while we're on the road."*

I was right to be concerned. But instead of using forces around us, like trees falling in our path or birds swooping into the windshield, the person in the silver car drove like a maniac.

She pulled in front of us then slammed on her brakes. Turning down a side street, we thought she was going another route until she made a complete circle and sped up behind us. She kept up with us for several blocks, weaving and swerving, speeding up then slamming on her brakes.

I couldn't panic. I whispered into Treacle's ear, keeping both hands on the wheel as my cat stared with wide green eyes out the window.

Finally, the silver car pulled away, and I hit the gas to get to Bea's house. It seemed like every car ride I took recently managed to take a couple of years off my life. This one was no exception.

Finally at my aunt's house, we all piled out of the car. Looking around, I noticed the street was quiet. Treacle strained and cried, trying to tear free of my arms. I knew he wanted me to let him go. I knew he missed prowling around on his own, but I couldn't be sure whether it was his idea or Jennifer's. I wasn't taking any chances. He had to stay with me.

"I know, Treacle. It won't be much longer." I held his big, squirming body as I tried to get to the front door.

"MEOW-MEOW-EROW!" He hissed, swiping at my face and clawing a long scratch down my neck. The mark quickly turned from a hot pink to a thin thread of bright red as blood surfaced.

I lost my grip on him, and he landed on the ground. With one push of his strong back legs, he was off, darting into the neighbor's yard, scooting underneath a car then out the other side to squeeze through a row of Yucca trees. Treacle had made his escape.

"Treacle!" I cried. My eyes burned instantly with tears. I took a few pathetic steps in the direction he'd run but knew I'd never be able to keep up with him, let alone catch him. "Oh, no! She's going to get him! She told me she would. She told me what she was going to do to him. To all of them. This is all my fault!"

"Come on." My aunt grabbed me by the hand. "She's doing this to distract you."

"No," I said pitifully. "She told me on the phone.

She said what she wanted and what she was going to do. She's calling him, and he's going to go to her. What have I done?"

Bea hurried and opened the door to her mother's house, tossing in a skinny and high-strung Peanut Butter. She quickly came back and scooped up Marshmallow.

"Cath, I know you're scared, but we don't have much time. If Treacle does go to her, then we need to find a way to get him back and get her in check. She's not playing by the rules. If she has your black cat, this might be a bigger fight than we anticipated."

"We?" I asked. "You guys can't come."

"Oh, right." Aunt Astrid stomped her way toward the house. "Bea, get the books from my nightstand. Cath, in the pantry behind the cans of soup, you'll find *The Outpost of the Enderton*. Grab that and—"

"I mean it. You guys can't come. I didn't tell her I'd meet her at the waterfall with my whole family. I just said me." I stood on the porch as my family stepped inside then turned to look at me. The image of us right there couldn't have been more perfect. Bea and her mom were inside the house, and I was standing at the threshold, on the porch but not in the house. It was so clear, I almost began to cry.

I didn't want to admit it, but although I'd never

felt unloved, I would always feel as if I were just outside the threshold. I don't believe my family made me feel that way. I chose it. I knew I would always feel like that, and I had taken a stick to that snakes' nest and poked and poked until every one of those tails rattled with hatred and aggression.

I couldn't risk my family. They'd have each other. How awful would I feel if I left one of them feeling like I did? What if I left one of them feeling incomplete, unfinished? I couldn't even think of it. It was too much.

"Do you think she's going to abide by that?" Aunt Astrid scowled. "Do you think she even knows the meaning of the words 'fair fight'? She killed a man for not being in love with her. How unreasonable is that? There is no telling what she'll do to you if she gets the upper hand."

I swallowed hard. "She won't."

"What time are you meeting her?" Aunt Astrid asked.

"I told her one in the morning. No one will be up there. Anyone around Lover's Lane would be long gone by then. No one else would get hurt."

"Fine," Aunt Astrid said. "Let's get to work, and no more talk about going solo."

I nodded without smiling or making eye contact.

I stepped over the threshold and felt a strange feeling of unfamiliarity. I wasn't sure if the feeling was real, or if Jennifer was getting her talons in me from a distance, or if I had just gotten myself so worked up that I didn't know what to feel.

Either way, I needed a plan, and hopefully there would be something in one of Aunt Astrid's books to help me. I hated the sense of loneliness I felt. Yet if I could prove to my aunt and cousin that I was capable of handling myself then maybe...

What was I thinking? Maybe this would somehow bring my parents back? Maybe all my years of growing up surrounded by oddities, curiosities, and just plain weirdness would pay off? Maybe this fight would prove I had the ability to get whatever took my mom and do what? Beat it up?

I was having trouble focusing. Why was I so distracted? I turned around and faced the street. In the distance, I saw a Wonder Falls police car cruise slowly by. Why wasn't Blake Samberg there to help?

What? Where in the world had that thought come from? I felt as though I'd spoken the words out loud, and both Aunt Astrid and Bea had heard me. I turned back to face them, my face beet red and my nerves a mess. This had to be some kind of inter-dimensional warfare. She had sprinkled some kind of fairy dust my way and was trying to get me so wrapped up in the wrong thoughts that I'd never be able to fight her.

"Cath, honey, she's working on you already. Come on." Bea took my hand like she did when we were little girls. I let her lead me into the house. Once Aunt Astrid shut the door, I looked around, almost surprised I was inside of the house. It was time to get to work… if I could just focus.

Dirty

✿❀✿

After several hours, I found myself starting to doze, which was not good considering I was stretched out on Aunt Astrid's couch, holding a four-inch thick book in front of my face.

Outside, the sky had gone from blue to violet to black, and the clock struck once, indicating ten thirty.

"Are you sure a good, old-fashioned binding spell won't do the trick on this one?" Bea asked, wiping her hair away from her face. She and my aunt had gone through two kettles of tea, and I had eaten three brownies I'd found in the back of the freezer.

"I'm just positive she'll be expecting that," Aunt Astrid said. "She has probably already put up her defenses and psychically bricked them over by now.

We need to find something that will enable Cath to fight fire with fire. And since Miss Skala has crossed so far into sorcery with no real knowledge of what she's doing based on her past handiwork, she's going to play dirty. Very dirty."

Dirty. The word stuck in my head, and I quietly got up, setting the big book down. Tucked on a shelf between some bigger books was just what I was looking for. I'd seen it before. It was about thirty pages long and reminded me of the CliffsNotes some kids used in high school when they didn't want to read a whole book. It was a classic witches' spell book called *Light Magic*... because it was so small.

I stuffed it into my back pocket, yawned, stretched, then shrugged. "Oh, geez!" I thought fast on my feet. "I think I'm still a little nauseated from those witches' vials." My lie was lame, but it was all I could think of.

Both Aunt Astrid and Bea looked at me as if I'd suddenly turned green.

I didn't say anything. I was sure they saw right through me. Then suddenly, my aunt jumped up from her seat, pushed aside the big book she was reading, and rushed over to me.

"You poor thing. You've got to rest. You can't have any distractions. It wasn't smart of you to challenge this woman, but I know your intentions were to save Treacle and us." My aunt tucked a few stray hairs behind my ear. "That's why we're going to help you. We'll find a spell that will work, something that will keep you safe and maybe, just maybe, knock her out of the game."

I looked deep into my aunt's eyes and saw how worried she was. It tore at my heart. I never lied to her. It made my stomach fold over on itself, and I thought I was going to start actually feeling like I did at Brit's place.

"Go lie down in my room. I'll have Bea bring you some special tea and—"

"No. I don't want any tea. Just a little rest. Maybe twenty minutes or so."

"Take a little longer than that if you need to," Bea said. "We'll be ready when it's time to go."

I couldn't look at them anymore. The guilt was too much. I looked down at my feet, smiled, and headed off to my aunt's room. Along the way, I grabbed a white candle and a book of matches from the side table in the hallway.

Once inside her room, I pulled out the little booklet and found exactly what I was looking for.

I said the words quietly over the tiny flame, lifting the spell to the four corners of the Earth and calling to my side a few familiar souls to walk with me on this scary journey.

I was scared for my family. More than that, I was scared for Treacle. He was out there, and I couldn't tell if it was because wandering was his nature, or if it was the hocus-pocus that Jennifer had cast on the felines around town. He was a tough kitty, but he was no match for that kind of black sorcery. He didn't stand a chance. And when it was all over, if she got a hold of him and did the horrible things she had threatened, he would just be left there, alone, dying, suffering, and wondering where I was.

My eyes clouded up with tears, but I continued my vigil, requesting the simplest assistance.

Once I was finished with part one, I tiptoed to the door and listened.

"Hmmm," I heard Bea mutter. "What about this? It's a chant to induce a sort of hologram. Cath wouldn't even have to actually go to the clearing. She could stay here in a circle of salt, but Jennifer would see her, hear her, yet not be able to touch her."

"Yes, yes, that sounds good. And here, look here," Bea said. "Since her strength would be at a lesser level, she could summon a simple silencing spell that would shut that girl's mouth for almost seventy-two hours. That would be just enough time for us to get a hold of her and make that muteness permanent. She wouldn't be able to summon a waiter, let alone a cessation spell."

"Do you think that would be enough? She is a murderer."

"We just have to stop her and trust that the universe will deal with her in an appropriate manner. It will be out of our hands by that point."

I shook my head. Why didn't I know about this omnipresent spell when I was taking gym class in high school, where it really would have come in handy? But this was a different situation.

Jennifer had threatened my family but had singled me out because of my cat... just like Darla had singled me out because something about me rubbed her the wrong way. I couldn't just send my shadow to fight. I had to be there no matter what my chances were. Anything other than a physical confrontation wasn't going to stop a person like Jennifer Skala. She thrived on inducing fear. Taking away her voice, even permanently, wasn't going to deter her. I had no doubt she would retaliate.

I looked at the clock and saw it was nearly eleven. I had to prepare, and if I was going through with meeting the class bully at the clearing by the top of the waterfall, I wanted to get there first. Hopefully, my little plan would work, and I could be back at my aunt's house soon and tell Aunt Astrid and Bea that Jennifer was no longer a problem. I quietly cracked the door and listened again.

"Why would Cath accept a fight like this? Without us? Without our help? She's never done anything like this before?" I could hear the hurt in Bea's voice. It made me feel worse than the lying did.

Aunt Astrid replaced the teakettle on the stove for the third time. The click, click, click of the burner kicking on sounded like a cricket from where I was standing.

"I don't know what she could be thinking, but we have to respect it. Although we're all family, she is still an orphan, and I don't think she'll ever not feel that desire to prove herself."

"She doesn't have to prove anything to us," Bea said. "Why would she think that?"

"Because she's so good. She doesn't want to be a burden or a victim or anything less than a true Greenstone woman. No matter how stubborn that may make her."

I'd heard enough. I had to leave and do this on my own. I quietly slipped out of the bedroom door, down the hallway, and to the front door.

Waterfalls

efore I could leave, I was confronted with Marshmallow, who stood there in all her puffed-up glory looking right at me. Behind her, Peanut Butter chased a rainbow prism on the ground that came from the lamp on my aunt's roll top desk.

"And where are you going?" Marshmallow asked.

"I'm going to get Treacle."

Marshmallow purred quietly. *"Take me with you."*

"No. And don't sound the alarm until I'm good and gone."

"Is it dangerous… what you're doing?"

"Yes."

"Will you come back?"

"I sure hope so."

Marshmallow rubbed up against my leg then stepped back, sitting on her haunches and looking at me through little slitted eyes. *"I'll be right here when you and Treacle come home."*

All I could do was smile. I opened the front door, slipped out, and pulled it tightly shut behind me.

The air felt colder than usual, and I wished I had a jacket. I would like to think the cold was what made me shake as I got into my car, started it up, and pulled out of the driveway without turning on the headlights. Once I was three houses away, I hit the lights and the gas and began my journey to the waterfall.

I saw a calico cat peering at me from the area of the woods where Treacle had run. Was the calico just a stray, or someone's furry companion out for an evening adventure? Or was it one of hers?

"It's not Treacle. There's still hope. That isn't him, and as long as I don't see him around, I can assume she doesn't have him. And if she doesn't, then she's just a hack witch with a bad attitude." The words sounded braver than I felt.

The dark street unfolded in front of me like an innocent set of rollercoaster tracks... the ones that led you up, up, up. They weren't threatening. There was nothing scary about those bits of track. The view was usually very pretty until you realized those tracks had led you to terror.

"Come on, Cath. You've got a plan. Stop freaking yourself out," I said out loud, hoping I'd listen to me and toughen up.

It usually took about twenty minutes to get to the waterfall clearing by car. If I wanted to play it extra safe, I'd park the car and take the path that, in the daytime, took about thirty minutes to maneuver. It was wide and well-marked, so I was pretty confident I would still get to the clearing before Jennifer with enough time to prepare.

I parked the car at a gravel turn-in where Wonder Falls Water Works vehicles and Wonder Falls Department of Streets and Sanitation trucks would park for their surveys and sometimes to nap. My car was barely visible from the street.

I grabbed a bottle of water that I had in the car and began to walk. The path was just ahead, and I was able to find it easily by the light from the streets. Once I was on it, though, the path became very dark, very fast.

The night was perfectly clear, and high in the sky,

a beautiful third-quarter moon seemed to welcome the millions of stars around it. Stopping for a moment, I listened and heard a wild and comforting choir of crickets. I was ready to start running if the sounds of nature stopped, but so far, it was just a regular night. Within minutes, I heard the sound of the waterfall in the distance. With each step, it grew louder and louder.

Finally, I saw the slope in the path begin to level out, and up ahead was the beautiful, flat clearing where the river lazily drifted past only to pick up speed in the distance in its hurry to get to the waterfall. The water wasn't that deep along the edges. Many people would stand on the bank in waders and fish. But the river did get deep in the center and at times, after the rains, the undertow would try to claim a victim or two.

Arriving at the center of the clearing, I knelt down. I began to finish the chant I had started at my aunt's house. This was part two, and I needed my hands in the dirt of this place, some water to mix, and just a couple of ancient words that were pretty to say and simple in concept. I wasn't looking for complicated.

I stood up, again greeting the four corners of the Earth with my hands covered in what was then sacred mud. I had one more step to complete but stopped dead in my tracks.

"Hey, who's over there?"

I knew that voice.

No.

Defensive

O f all the times and places, Blake Samberg had to show up then.

"Blake?" I said in a hushed voice. "Is that you?"

"Cath Greenstone?" I heard his voice and suddenly saw a spot from a small flashlight not twenty feet from me. "What are you doing up here at this hour?" he asked, strolling my way.

"I thought there was supposed to be a meteor shower tonight. I came up here to get a front row seat, so to speak," I said nervously as the flashlight lit up almost everything around me. "But you can't see a thing with that flashlight. Maybe you should douse it, you know?"

"No, you won't miss anything. It's next week.

Actually, Jake said this was a good place for stargazing. I didn't know you were interested in astronomy." He shifted from his left foot to his right as he stood close to me. The soft glow of the flashlight lit his face, and I noticed what looked like a smile on his face.

"You have no idea." I looked up at the stars that had helped me find my way home on more than one occasion, as well as fight a demon once. That was another long story for another time. "I think I'll be going now."

"I didn't see a car pull up. Did you take the path up here?" Blake asked. He sure was talkative.

"Yes. I felt like walking, sort of taking the path less traveled, you know? But I think I'll be heading back now."

"Well, let me give you a ride."

"No. That's not necessary."

"You don't want to walk that path in the dark. You could slip and fall." He shined his flashlight on me and saw my hands covered in mud. "Or did you already?"

I held them up in front of me, shrugging.

"Yeah, you know how clumsy I am. Just ask Bea." It was all I could think of to say.

"All the more reason you shouldn't walk back."

"Look, I know you're trying to help, but I don't need any help."

"From the looks of it, you really do."

"This isn't the time or place, Blake, for you to get all police-y on me. I'm a big girl. It isn't a crime to fall in the mud."

"Why are you getting so defensive?"

"I'm not defensive."

"You sound like it."

"Well, that shows how much you know. Now, if you don't mind, I'd like to wash my hands in the water and be on my way."

"Leaning over the banks at night is also dangerous. Let me get you a bottle of water from the car, and you can wash your hands with that."

"Fine. If it will make you happy."

"It would. Just wait here."

I watched as Blake's flashlight bounced along the ground a good couple of yards from where I was standing. Quickly, I hurried to the water's edge. No sooner was I on my knees, bent down, and reaching for the water, than I heard another familiar voice.

"Isn't this nice?" Her voice was low and menacing, like the growl of a hungry animal. "You get here early and bring the police."

I whipped around and got to my feet. My hands

were still caked with mud. I just needed a drop, one single drop from the river to complete my spell. But Jennifer had other ideas. I quickly stepped to the side to get myself in between Jennifer and Blake.

"He was here when I got here. Leave him out of it." I tried to appeal to her logical side, if she had one. "He's a cop. You don't want to be known as a cop killer," I said, making a design in the dirt with my foot.

"What is that you're doing? Some kind of binding spell?"

If I lived through this ordeal, I'd be sure to tell Aunt Astrid she'd nailed that one. Miss Paranoia would have sniffed out a binding spell from thirty miles away.

"No." I quickly glanced behind me in the direction Blake had walked. I still saw the light from his flashlight aimed away from me and in the trunk of his car.

"What are you looking for? Did you bring other people here, too? Maybe Brit is with you or your aunt. Who's back there besides that cop?"

I didn't say anything. I was trying to concentrate and find the right words. But when Jennifer stepped closer to me, I saw her face clearer than I'd ever wanted to.

Her cheeks were high and chiseled. Her mouth was covered in thick, red lipstick, and her eyes were plain, milky white holes in her face. I couldn't help but gasp.

"I'll tear you to shreds," she hissed.

"Cath? You okay?" Blake yelled.

"Do not keep until the frost. Time to sleep when time is lost," I muttered quickly, pointing in the direction Blake had called from. Within a few seconds, I heard the gentle thud of a body hitting the ground. He was asleep. His catnap would last a little while and buy me some time.

"Your boyfriend?"

My cheeks flushed. Anger surged through me because I knew even in the dark, Jennifer could feel my embarrassment, and she enjoyed it.

But I had to stay in control. My plan was so simple, and all I needed was some water and a little luck.

I started to inch my way toward the riverbank but was frozen in place when Jennifer grinned a wide grimace of sharpened teeth. The moon bounced off of them and gave her an almost translucent look. She growled a low, feral-sounding grunt, and I began to shake.

"I'll tear you apart, but only after I have my fun with that man married to your cousin."

Jake. No!

"I'll drive his wife mad. Hearing noises, seeing things, and late-night visitations from some of the more aggressive entities should send her off the deep end quite nicely."

"You stay away from my family!"

"Well, aren't you scary?" She waved her hand, and I felt as if I had just been punched in the gut. I reeled backward only to lose my balance and fall on my butt. I coughed and gagged. She came at me again, clenching her fist. I felt my hair being pulled by the handfuls, and I was dragged up to Jennifer's face.

"Is this all you've got?" I asked. "I thought you were supposed to be some kind of super witch. All you're doing is beating me up without using your hands. Any sixth-grader could do that."

She snarled at me, her lips peeling back from her horrible teeth. Why had she done that to herself? I was reminded of the before and after pictures of drug addicts, except Jennifer depicted what sorcery did to a person. It was black, no matter what anyone said.

If Bea were there and took Jennifer's hand, she would probably see the black lesions in her brain…

layers and layers of filth, clogging up her arteries and coating her organs like a parasite. But unlike a cancer or a tumor, paranormal infections are invited in. Jennifer had made an intentional transformation, and she was enjoying herself.

I was tossed another fifteen feet across the grass. I lay there panting, wondering what time it was and why the hell I hadn't allowed my family to come and help. I almost laughed out loud at the thought, but it couldn't get past the lump in my throat when I heard the most horrible sound.

Trying to gulp in air enough to speak, I croaked out the word. "Treacle?"

It was a quiet meow, but I heard it.

"NO!" I screamed in my head. *"Run, Treacle! Hide. Don't come here!"* But I got no answer.

"Aren't you going to even try and fight back? Don't you have a power of any kind, or are you one of those witches who can only make flowers grow or talk to animals?" Jennifer laughed. Her white eyes scrunched into half moons as her cheeks pushed them up.

I tried muttering a spell of confusion to get her lost for a few minutes, even seconds, so I could get to the water. My head pounded, and my stomach and ribs ached terribly. But when I muttered the words, I felt the psychic vibration as it bounced right off of her. I tried a binding spell again, which was all I could think of at the moment, but it also rolled off of her like raindrops on a windshield.

Suddenly, I was yanked to my feet. Jennifer held me by my collar with one hand. She walked toward the riverbank, and my feet dragged clumsily along the ground.

"Your family will probably find your body in a couple days. And you know what the autopsy will say? Natural causes. Who would have thought someone so young, so full of life, would have such a bad ticker." She swung me over the edge, bending my back at an unnatural angle.

I looked around as best I could and saw a sleek, black form moving along the grass.

Three Flashes

꧁꧂

"*G*et away, Treacle!" I screamed in my head. "*Run home! Just get home where it's safe!*" I then saw him rub against Jennifer's leg. My eyes swelled with tears. She had him, and she was going to kill him, slowly and cruelly. My mud-crusted hand clutched her, and I sank my nails in as far as I could. "*Fight her, Treacle! Remember me? I wouldn't hurt you! Fight her!*"

"Oh, I see. I got your cat," Jennifer said. "He's been lurking around here for a little while now while you've been doing anything but fighting back. He's seen you give up. Now he's mine."

I coughed and cried, still clawing at her hand around my neck. I was starting to feel light-headed.

With one last try, I screamed in my head, *"One good swipe, Treacle!"*

I think the balance between the light and the darkness had been tipped because just as I thought I was going to pass out, I heard a fierce *meower-er-eow*.

My cat hissed and arched his back with all his fur on edge. In one sudden movement, he jumped up at Jennifer's face.

She screamed out a stream of obscenities as Treacle scratched all the way down her cheek. She dropped me to the ground, and I landed on the hard, bumpy rocks that were along the banks of the river. Just as I looked up, she waved her left hand, and my poor cat went flying into a tree, dropping to the ground with a thud.

As much as my gut pulled me toward Treacle, I reached out to the water instead. I just needed one lousy drop. Then I heard Jennifer again. She just wouldn't shut up.

"I'll kill you both! I'll tear you apart! You'll explode from the inside out just like the others!"

I scrambled with all my strength just to get a couple more inches, but Jennifer had me in her invisible vise. I felt my breath catch in my chest. My whole body was in pain, and my chest was burning.

I arched backward, and with my last ounce of free

will, I stretched toward the water only inches away, but it seemed like miles. My muddy hand came closer and closer to the slow-moving ripples. Finally, I felt the cold water gently kiss the very tip of my fingers, and I muttered the words, *"Coerce an unblemished soul for infinity, and let this be washed away."*

The water in the lake shot up into a fine spray. It seemed as though it went all the way up to the stars, but that may have been because the oxygen had stopped going to my brain for several minutes.

Jennifer was soaked from head to toe, and so was I. But I saw what I'd hoped to see. The Maid of the Mist.

The thing about the Maid of the Mist is that she didn't always show up when you needed her. She showed up when she felt like it, when the cause was worthy, and when her absence would cause more harm than good.

With each drop of cold water on Jennifer's skin, the residue of the black magic she'd been wallowing in was washed off. She didn't know it. She didn't feel it. But the enchanted water of the Maid of the Mist had the power to wash away what had been accumulated through false and misguided methods.

If Jennifer were a real sorceress, someone with a bloodline tied to it, then this cleansing ritual wouldn't have worked. But she was a wannabe, a hack, a freshman self-taught in the diabolical. And the diabolical had no real use for an amateur witch.

"Great! You splashed me!" Jennifer said, unaware her powers had left her.

Her eyes were still filled with hatred for me. She waved a hand, expecting to see something. When she did it again and nothing happened, her eyes became wild. She looked as if she had just emerged from a cave, with her hair straggling in a hundred different directions and her teeth gritted together.

I slowly regained my composure and looked toward where Treacle had smashed into the tree. I began to hobble in that direction.

"Stop!" Jennifer yelled. I paid no attention to her. She was just a person... a regular person with no special talents for causing heart attacks, or making people fall to the ground, or punching someone in the stomach with invisible fists.

I wanted my cat to be all right. I wanted Treacle back to the way he was.

"Stop!" she yelled again. As if something snapped, she began swearing and stomping her feet. Waving her arms, she found no magic there. She looked like a person suffering from an epileptic fit of some kind. I couldn't watch. Instead, I carefully got down on my hands and knees. Crawling through the grass, I felt for Treacle. In my head, I was screaming for him. Tears rolled down my cheeks. Then I heard it.

"I'm here." His voice was so little, but I heard it. Within seconds, I felt his warm fur beneath my hand.

"Are you hurt badly?"

"I don't think so," he said weakly, letting me scoop him up into my arms and hold him close. *"It was like a nightmare in there. Her mind pushed into mine. It hurt. It was so black."*

"I'm so sorry," I said aloud.

"Do you think I care if you're sorry?"

I whipped around to see Jennifer standing just a few feet from us. In the moonlight, I could see she had one thing no witch could stop with just magic. She had a gun. I couldn't speak.

"What have you done to me? I'll kill you for this! I don't need witchcraft for that! I'll kill you and—"

"Put the gun down!" I heard Blake call out.

Jennifer's face was shadowed, but she looked nervously to her left where Blake's voice was coming from.

"Just put the gun down, Miss."

He approached with his gun drawn and his flashlight trained on Jennifer.

She began to wave her hands and utter spells in long-dead languages that I wouldn't dare say out loud. Without knowing what she had done, she had allowed the blackest sorcery into her body and soul. When it was removed, the damage had already been done. She was insane. "You deserve to die like Marvin! Like Lucas! Like Bob and Regina! You'll pay for this, too."

"Who's Bob and Regina?" I asked, clutching Treacle close to me, feeling his warm, purring body and stroking his fur nervously.

"Put the gun down!" Blake cried out.

"…deserve to die."

"I'm not going to tell you again!"

"I'll kill you!"

"Miss! Put the gun down!"

It was then that all the crickets stopped. I saw three flashes—one from Jennifer's direction and two from Blake's.

My shoulder felt as if it had burst into flames, and Treacle jumped from my arms. I collapsed to my knees then fell over. Everything was so quiet except for Blake's voice. I heard him request an ambulance.

I heard him say two people were down. Was I one of them?

The grass was cool against my cheek when I turned my head. My shoulder felt hot and cold at the same time. And it was wet. Something hot and wet was seeping through my shirt. My mind wasn't thinking correctly. I should have just kept my mouth shut when Blake came to me.

His strong arms slipped underneath my head and back. He held my shoulder tightly. It hurt yet felt comforting. "You're okay, Cath. I promise. You're okay," he said softly. "The ambulance is on its way. You're going to be just fine."

"I'm glad you're here," I muttered as I looked up into his face. I saw what looked like a kind smile. "I'm always glad you're here." I would remember seeing all the stars behind his head.

"I am, too," he said.

After that, it was darkness.

Celestial Delights

✦

When I finally woke up, I was in a bright room with flowers and wolf bane in pretty vases all around. I blinked my eyes a few times and tried to sit up, but my shoulder screamed out in a sharp, jagged pain.

"Ouch," I whimpered.

"Oh, my gosh! For heaven's sake, don't move! You've been shot. Take it easy," Bea said in her most motherly voice. Had I closed my eyes, she would have sounded just like Aunt Astrid. I looked up to see she had been crying.

"What's the matter? Did I almost die?" I asked with a mouth as dry as the desert.

"What's the matter? You hear that, Mom? What's the matter? You go off and fight the Wicked Witch of

Insanity all by yourself and get shot and then ask what's the matter?"

The whole ordeal came rushing back. Not only had I been shot in the shoulder, I had one heck of a magic burnout, too. "Yeah, in hindsight, I guess it wasn't such a great idea."

"No, it wasn't," Aunt Astrid scolded. "However, a cleansing ritual—how practical. We were too busy trying to stoop to her level, and here you were taking the high road. You made us very proud."

"I don't feel proud. How is she?"

Neither Bea nor my aunt needed to answer. I saw the looks on their faces and knew Jennifer had died.

Bea climbed onto the side of the bed and took my hand in hers. "She was sick, Cath. There was no medicine that was ever going to cure her. No therapy that would have brought her back."

"Detective Samberg doesn't realize it because he is such a good man, but he helped her more than any one of us ever could have," Aunt Astrid said. "Before she got to Marvin, she was wanted in New York City for the murder of a ten-year-old boy and his mother. She drove right into them at a crosswalk. Video footage makes it look like it was deliberate."

"How awful. A sacrifice obviously." I winced at the pain in my shoulder.

Bea nodded, still holding my hand and patting it as though I were a child with a fever.

"It was really divine intervention that Blake was there to begin with," Aunt Astrid said. "How lucky for all of us that he was."

I felt my cheeks blush as my aunt talked about him in such glowing terms.

"And…" Bea grinned like the cat that swallowed the canary. "He said you said you were glad he was here in town."

"I didn't say that."

"Sure you did."

"No, I said something like 'glad you're here to help me with this bullet in my shoulder.'"

"That's not what Jake said Blake said."

"No. I said I was glad he was there at that moment. Otherwise, well, I'd be dead."

Bea looked suspiciously at my aunt as if they had some insider knowledge about me.

"Blake needs to get his ears cleaned out," I muttered, my eyebrows pursed together in aggravation.

"Knock, knock!" Jake said, as he walked in carrying a big box of chocolates and some crossword puzzle books. "How's our girl feeling?" He leaned down to give me a kiss on the forehead then quickly peck Bea on the lips.

"I'm doing fine."

"That was quite a stunt you pulled. Your aunt and your cousin won't yell at you because they're just happy you're all right, but you had all of us worried sick. Bea called me up half-hysterical that you'd left the house without telling them."

"I'm sorry?" I said as more of a question than a statement because I wasn't sure if Jake was serious. Not until I looked into his eyes and saw the tears. Then I proceeded to feel horrible.

"You better be," the big man said, folding his huge arms in front of his chest.

"I promise I'll never go out and engage in a conversation or beat-down with anyone who is mentally unstable."

Jake nodded then gave me a wink.

I smiled back and tried not to move too much.

"They told you the news about Jennifer, right?" he asked.

"Yes."

Just then, there was another knock on the door.

"Oh, come in, Detective!" Aunt Astrid rushed across the hospital room to the door. "Please do come in."

I saw that Blake was carrying a paper bag

with some big thing in it. He must have been there to visit someone else and was bringing that person a package. He didn't smile, even when Aunt Astrid hugged him. Instead, he looked around the room as if he were planning his escape.

"Hello." He nodded.

Jake walked over to shake his hand and pull him a little farther into the room.

"Hmm," Bea said quietly in my ear. "I feel your pulse has gone up. What could possibly be causing that?"

I pulled my hand away from Bea and wrinkled my nose at her.

"How are you feeling?" Blake asked, still standing almost in the doorway.

"I'm okay."

"You shouldn't have been out there alone. Statistics show women who are out past a certain time of night are seventy-five percent more likely to—"

"Well, I'm a big girl. I can go out when I want to."

"You might want to consider purchasing some Mace."

"I'll take that under consideration."

"There are also self-defense classes at the station."

"Will you be there?"

"No."

"Well, then maybe I'll check it out."

"That would be wise."

"Okay."

"Okay."

"Fine."

"Okay."

After Blake and I managed to make everyone in the room uncomfortable, they all decided to head down to the cafeteria for a snack and some coffee. Blake hung back for a few minutes. "I picked this up for you. The doctor said you'd be out in a day or two, but you should probably rest as much as they'll let you."

"Well, you didn't have to do that," I said, trying to be nice. "In fact, if anyone owes someone a gift, I owe you."

He stood a little closer to the bed, looking down at his shoes and gently touching the edge of the blanket by my feet. He kept shaking his head, but I continued.

"Look, I know you don't really like me. I'm a

little prickly, I know. But from the bottom of my heart, thank you. I owe you one."

"No, you don't."

"Yes, I do."

"No, really, I was just doing my job."

"I know, but it's hard on you, too."

"It's okay."

"Really."

"You're welcome." He stood around for a few more awkward minutes then turned to face me. "I've got to get back to the office. I've got a lot of paperwork."

"Oh," I said, reluctant to admit I felt a little disappointment. "Well, thanks for stopping by."

Blake nodded. Without a smile, he handed me the package in a paper bag that he'd been carrying, then in three strides of his long legs, he walked out. I waited, hoping that maybe he'd come back. But he didn't. I was all alone.

I reached in the bag and pulled out the gift inside. It was a book.

Celestial Delights: The Best Astronomical Events Through 2030.

About the Author

Harper Lin is a *USA TODAY* bestselling cozy mystery author. When she's not reading or writing mysteries, she loves going to yoga classes, hiking, and hanging out with her family and friends.

www.HarperLin.com